A Doctor BLIND DATE for the COWBOY

dobi daniels

Luxhaven
Publishing

ISBN paperback, 978-1-958987-14-8

Interior Design by Luxhaven Publishing

Cover Design by The Book Brander Boutique

Editing by JD Book Services

Proofreading by Lisa Lee Proofreading

To JC, Grandma D, and DC, whom I love more than life itself.

AUTHOR'S NOTE

Thank you for choosing A DOCTOR BLIND DATE FOR THE COWBOY. I enjoyed writing the story of Zoey Brown and Dex Dexin, two very fun characters!

It's so easy to believe you'd never get a chance at love or that circumstances beyond your control would limit your ability to find love. I pray A DOCTOR BLIND DATE FOR THE COWBOY gives you hope to believe that love is still possible no matter your circumstances.

Please continue this journey with me in A DOCTOR ENEMY FOR THE COWBOY, which is the story of how Dex's brother, Rex, found love. You can grab your copy at https://dobidaniels.com.

Would you like to be notified when the next Dobi Daniels book releases? Sign up at https://dobidaniels.com.

Once again, thank you so much for purchasing A DOCTOR BLIND DATE FOR THE COWBOY and for meeting Jasmine Banks and David Landi. If you enjoyed it, please consider leaving a review at your favorite retailer or recommending it to a friend.

Thanks again for your support!

Dobi Daniels

A Doctor

BLIND DATE

for the COWBOY

CHAPTER 1

oey Brown froze, her face warming up more than the hot Saturday sun she'd just walked in from. How could this have happened to her today of all days?

"Ma'am, your skirt is ripped," the cool baritone voice repeated quietly behind her.

Zoey bristled even as the scented smell of cleaning supplies from the nearby detergent aisle assaulted her nostrils. Yes, she'd heard him the first time. Did he have to repeat it again? She fought the urge to reach back and touch the rip that had appeared as she'd leaned forward to place her groceries on the checkout counter.

It served her right. She should have just stuck with the pants and jeans that had been her uniform for over a decade. Instead, she'd opted for a black skirt and a sleeveless peach blouse, which went wonderfully with her sun-kissed skin, for a change. Today's weather forecast had predicted it would be the hottest day of summer. Who knew the universe would reward her efforts with this unwanted publicity on her first day in Dexin Valley?

Zoey bit her lip. She couldn't continue standing here, pretending nothing was wrong. How was she going to get herself out of this pickle? Her jacket was in her car, too far away to reach without taking a walk of shame through the store and out into the parking lot. How could she deal with this in the gracious manner her stepmother liked to harp on without becoming the day's side show in the tiny grocery store that seemed to be serving half of the town's population right now?

She could feel the curious gazes from the other shoppers around her. It didn't help that this was the day she'd decided to wear her comfy white granny underwear instead of the more sophisticated lingerie that filled her wardrobe. Now all it did was serve as a white flag against the contrasting black skirt, calling attention to the tear.

Something fell on Zoey's shoulders, and she flinched. She looked down only to see a dark brown plaid shirt—long enough to extend beyond the hem of her skirt—resting on her shoulders. It carried the faint scent of sweet hay, leather, and fresh grass, a fragrance that seemed to warm her more than the shirt itself.

Zoey turned in relief to see who the owner was, and her eyes met the warmest brown eyes she'd ever seen—twin mirrors that seemed to reach down into her soul. The broad-chested young man towered over her five-foot-seven frame, and his eyes held a look of concern as they searched her face.

"Hope you don't mind, ma'am," he said in the same voice she'd heard earlier, gesturing to the shirt. "Are you okay?"

So he'd been the one to notice her skirt! He was now clad in a white V-necked T-shirt and very dark blue jeans. A brown cowboy hat sat at a careless angle on his head. His boots looked worn, like they'd survived many winters, yet they seemed to be made with the finest craftsmanship she'd ever seen in a pair of work boots, with their beautiful detailed multi-color contrast stitching.

But Zoey couldn't allow herself to be distracted by how fine he looked. Even though he'd helped solve her immediate predicament, it was best to leave the grocery store before any further accidents happened with her skirt. She also needed to return his shirt as soon as possible.

She looked up at him. "Yes, I'm fine," she said. "Thanks for the shirt." Some of the other shoppers who'd watched their exchange had already lost interest and were now moving along. But that didn't mean Zoey was out of the woods yet.

"Happy to help, ma'am," he responded.

Now what was up with all the "ma'ams" when she obviously looked younger than him?

"Ma'am, your bags," the young cashier that had been attending to her said.

Zoey's face felt impossibly hot. Well, it appeared this "ma'am" thing was endemic to the store. The alternative—that she looked much older than her age —was unacceptable.

She turned back to the cashier. "Thank you," she said as she picked up her bags. Then her eyes swung back to the tall gentleman. "Do you mind following me to my car?" she said. "I'd like to return your shirt."

"You can keep it if you like," he replied. "It's no bother."

Zoey shook her head. "Thank you, but I'd prefer to return it if you don't mind."

He stared at her for a moment as if trying to decipher her thoughts. "Okay," he finally said. "Let me help you with your bags then."

"No, thank you," Zoey said. "I can handle them myself."

He chuckled. "I can tell you're new to the area. Here, we gentlemen help ladies with their bags." As if anticipating her continued protest: "And what if the shirt falls off your shoulders?"

Zoey's ears burned. Why did he have to call attention back to the rip? Though she had to admit he had a point. If the shirt dropped and she had to bend to pick it up, she could end up arrested for flashing! "Okay, you can help," she conceded.

He reached for the bags, and as Zoey handed them over, their fingers brushed. Zoey felt a spark of electricity zap through her arm, and she jerked it back in shock.

"Are you alright, ma'am?" he asked.

So he probably hadn't felt the buzz. Why had she reacted this way to a total stranger?

She tucked in her upper lip. Maybe it had merely been a figment of her imagination. But it unsettled her nonetheless. "I'm okay," she said as much for herself as for him.

Zoey hurried out of the store before her face betrayed her confusion. She could hear his footsteps behind her, much lighter than she would have expected from a man as well-built as he was. Yes, she'd noticed. Only a blind bat wouldn't have seen his well-honed physique that even his T-shirt couldn't hide.

Get yourself together, Zoey, she thought. She was only here from New York to check out Dexin Valley's new ER Center at the behest of Tara, her best friend from medical school, who'd dropped by Zoey's apartment and gushed about the town.

"I bet you'll love it there," Tara had said as she sat crosslegged on Zoey's twin-sized bed tucked into a corner of her tiny West End studio. "Dexin Valley is so picturesque from what I hear. Lots of fresh air and not too far from here or Boston. You've always wished to work in a place where the pace of life was slower. Nothing is stopping you from going for it now, since you're done with your ER fellowship."

Zoey had just completed her Emergency Medicine fellowship at one of New York's leading hospitals and had received a few offers for Assistant Professorship spots from hospitals in New York, Boston, and even faraway California. She'd turned down the California offer, as the terms of their contract had been inflexible, and was currently in negotiations with the Boston and New York hospitals, though their bureaucratic wheels had slowed the process as expected. It was mostly a waiting game for her at this point.

So Zoey's interest had been piqued. "It sounds nice," she'd said.

"But the best part I hear are the cute, polite cowboys who live in the area," Tara teased. "You've always had a thing for cowboys."

Zoey's face burned hotly. "I do not."

Tara chuckled. "You don't have to pretend. I saw the photo. You know, the one in the special box you keep tucked away at the back of your closet. He's cute."

Zoey blinked. "How–"

"Don't get mad. I was looking for that clutch you'd offered to lend me, and the picture fell out from the box. I'm sorry I invaded your privacy, but it wasn't intentional. You guys looked great together."

Zoey's throat tightened. She wasn't sure why she still held onto that picture, not when she hadn't seen him for a very long time. "It's nothing. We were kids."

"He's—"

"I don't want to talk about it."

Tara raised her hands in surrender. "Okay, okay,

I'll back off now. But, seriously, you'd love it there. Dexin Valley, I mean."

Zoey crossed her legs as she reclined in the only chair in the room. The idea sounded interesting. She'd grown up in Texas before her family had moved to New York, and she sometimes wished to be away from the bustle of life here. Still, there were things only the city could give her. "I need to work with more established doctors for a few years to gain more experience. That won't be a possibility in a place like that."

Tara grinned before responding. "That shouldn't be a problem. I hear they have an agreement with Dexington Medical and are also hiring the best doctors from around the country. Seriously, you should totally apply before they stop hiring." Dexington Medical was a premier hospital network in the northeast region. It was a big deal if Dexin Valley had an agreement with them.

But Zoey wasn't totally convinced. "I'll think about it."

"Good. Now what's for dinner?"

The discussion had then turned to the hottest new restaurants in New York.

But Zoey hadn't forgotten about the conversation, and now here she was, two weeks later, scouting the area and meeting with the Director of the ER Center for an interview. She'd taken a long overdue vacation and planned to spend the next two weeks exploring the area. Zoey had only stopped by the grocery store to pick up a few items she needed for her stay before heading to the bed and breakfast she'd rented. Instead, she'd ended up with a ripped skirt.

So this wasn't the time to be checking out eligible bachelors. It would only be a big distraction, and she wasn't interested in relationships—they only brought pain in the end. She was here to see if the Dexin ER Center was worth pursuing and nothing more. Well, and to also confirm that Dexin Valley was as beautiful as Tara had made it out to be. So far, the latter seemed to be true from what she'd seen on her way into town. But that didn't change what her top priority was, and she had to stay focused on that alone.

She reached her car and pulled out the fall jacket from the back seat. It would suffice for now, until she had a chance to change out of her outfit. Zoey shrugged off the man's shirt and donned the jacket. Then she handed the shirt back to him. "Thank you," she said. "Sorry to have been a bother."

"You're welcome. It was nothing," he replied as he accepted his shirt.

An awkward silence reigned for a moment. A part of her wanted to ask him his name. But she'd been embarrassed enough for one day and figured it was best to put the incident behind her as soon as possible. "Well, have a good day," she finally said.

"You too, ma'am," the man said, tipping his hat at her.

She hurried over to the driver's side, but he'd somehow managed to get there before her and now held the door open for her.

Nice. It had been a long while since she'd experienced this western chivalry, and she had to admit she still liked every bit of it. That said, nothing good could come from associating with a man who had witnessed one of her most embarrassing moments, even if he looked like a much-needed tall drink of water on this hot summer day.

Zoey entered her car. The man closed the door for her and stepped back. She turned the ignition, put the car into drive, and sped off.

And fought the urge to look back at the man she'd left behind.

Zoey prayed they'd never meet again.

CHAPTER 2

*D*ex Dexin stood in the parking lot with the harsh afternoon sun beating down on his skin and watched as the car drove away, the lady with the beautiful dark wavy hair at its wheel. She'd done a good job of remaining calm in the midst of what had surely been an embarrassing situation. Something about her connected with him, though he couldn't put his finger on what it was.

He'd been headed to the detergent aisle when he'd noticed the lady standing alone in line at the checkout counter with a glaring rip in the back of her skirt. A few other customers in the store seemed to have spotted it as well.

Dex's first instinct had been to ignore and move on—he didn't need an accusation of sexual harassment just for noticing her dilemma. But then he'd imagined how Becca, his sister-in-law, might have felt if she was the one in that situation. So he'd gone up to her and dropped his shirt around her.

He was sure they'd never met before—he would have recalled her heart-shaped face and pert nose—and he'd never seen her around town. Maybe she was just passing through. There had been a lot more foot traffic in town lately, especially with the construction of the ER Center, which Dex's brother, Max, had founded. Dex wasn't certain if this was to be the new normal.

Of course, he'd been expecting the change for some time now, though he'd only noticed the transition recently. Dex was in charge of the day-to-day operations of the ranch he co-owned with his brothers, which meant a full daily schedule and a rare chance to come into town. Still, he considered it a shift in the right direction.

As much as he loved his town, it was time for an injection of new blood in the area. Not that his motives were entirely altruistic. Dex had started to yearn for a family of his own, and none of the local ladies had caught his interest. They were wonderful women in their own right, but some loved the romantic idea of marrying a cowboy—not the reality of it. Dex needed a woman who made his heart skip a beat, one that loved him for who he was and not the name he represented, someone who appreciated his hands that worked the land, and who was willing to settle on a ranch with him.

Because, unlike his brothers, Dex knew the land and him were one. He could feel its heartbeat, knew this was his calling, and couldn't imagine living anywhere else. He wanted someone who would embrace him wholeheartedly, a person he could give his all to and trust it would be treasured.

Sure, he wasn't as outgoing and smart as Jax, his other brother, or as handsome as Max, and he was more introverted than any of the other members of his family, yet Dex had a heart full of love to offer and treasured his family and God above everything else. Yet he had to be careful not to entrust his heart to the wrong person.

Maybe it was best for him to focus on the boot-making mentoring program with the Weston Brothers he'd been preparing to apply for in the last few months. The submission deadline was coming up soon. The Weston Brothers were leaders in the custom bootmaking world, and their boots currently boasted a three-year waitlist.

If Dex was selected for this opportunity, he'd get

the rare chance to learn from two of the world's top masters in this field. It would open more doors for him in a hobby he loved, and maybe it would eventually turn into something more. The Weston Brothers mentored one aspiring bootmaker every two years and sometimes chose none if they didn't find what they were looking for. Dex hoped he'd be selected this time around.

But enough dawdling. He still needed to pick up some detergent for Becca as well as other groceries. Maggie, his foster mom who'd run the household for many years, was on her honeymoon with her new husband, Peter. Becca wasn't much of a homemaker and had her hands full with five-year-old Chloe, so Dex had taken control of the kitchen until Maggie returned. It was time for him to take care of business and then head home. He still had work to do around the ranch.

Dex turned and strode back to the store. As he reached its entrance, he saw Miss Prissy, Maggie's longtime friend and the owner of a popular restaurant in town, pushing a cart out through the parted sliding glass doors, her sunglasses perched on top of her silvery short bob. The smell of fresh bread and coffee followed her out.

"Good afternoon, Miss Prissy," Dex said, tipping his hat at her.

She looked up and flashed him a smile. "Hello, Dex," she said. "Just the man I wanted to see."

"*Me*?" Miss Prissy had never asked to see him in all the years he'd known her, which was a very long time. "What can I do for you, ma'am?"

"Well, I'm sure you must have heard that I opened a matchmaking business. Bought a weekly column in the local newspaper too."

Dex raised his eyebrows. Matchmaking? Sure, Miss Prissy was the biggest gossip in town, and her restaurant was a well-known fountain of information. One only had to spend a few hours there to be up-to-date on the latest news in town—it still baffled Dex how the town's newspaper made any money with Miss Prissy around. But it was a big leap to go from being the town's best cook and gossip to opening a matchmaking business. "I haven't," he said.

Miss Prissy stared at him quizzically. "Really? Becca didn't tell you?"

"Tell me what, ma'am?" Dex was only half-listening and was keen to move on to the grocery shopping he still had to do. Experience had taught him never to hang around Miss Prissy for too long, else he might end up parting with some information that could become the latest news in town.

"The column in the newspaper will feature an eligible bachelor or lady each week, and folks who are interested will respond to the column and book a blind date with him or her," Miss Prissy said. "Of course, we'll vet each individual to make sure everything is on the up and up. But I'm so glad you've agreed to grace the maiden edition. We've already gotten a record amount of folks responding to your profile."

Dex's heart jerked in his chest. Wait! What? His profile? He didn't recall agreeing to anything of the sort. Dex was a very private person and didn't care for publicity of any kind, so he was pretty certain he hadn't given his consent. "What are you talking about?" he insisted.

An elderly farmer who owned a couple of acres next to Dex's ranch passed them on his way into the store. "Looking good, Dex," the man said, patting Dex on the shoulder.

"He does, right?" Miss Prissy called after him.

Dex pinched the bridge of his nose. This wasn't some random joke—this was real. But how?

"Becca didn't tell you? I mentioned it to her last week and asked that she pass the message to you, but she said it was fine and that you wouldn't mind." Miss Prissy must have seen something on his face, because she said: "Oh, my! I hope this isn't a big problem." She searched her bag and pulled out a newspaper clipping. "Here. This is a copy of the column."

Dex accepted the folded paper and flipped it open to see a smiling picture of himself staring back at him. The picture had been taken during Max and Becca's wedding reception, one of the few times he'd let down his guard around folks that weren't family.

His nostrils flared. How could Becca have submitted his picture without his consent? She should have known better about his opinions on things like this. Now nothing could reverse it since it was already published. This newspaper feature could be why folks had been extra friendly to him since he'd entered the store. Yet he'd been the only fool who hadn't known.

Dex took a deep breath to calm himself so as not to hurt Miss Prissy's feelings. Maggie would have his hide if he did. "It's fine," he said, handing the clipping back to her.

Miss Prissy let out a relieved sigh. "Good. I was worried there for a moment." She slipped the paper back into her bag. "I'll contact you with the details once everything is all set." She adjusted her sunglasses over her eyes. "I have to go now before Connie sends someone after me." Connie was Miss Prissy's niece who worked with her at the bed and breakfast she also ran.

"Let me help you with your cart," Dex said.

Miss Prissy waved him away. "There's no need for that. Bob will handle it." Indeed, Bob—a widower who'd been sweet on Miss Prissy since forever—was headed in their direction, his long legs eating up the distance. With how often they were together, Dex sometimes wondered why they never got married.

"Have a good day, ma'am," Dex said, tipping his hat to her and watching as she headed to Bob's car. Then he pulled out his phone and called Becca.

It rang through. He tried again but with no success. Since he considered this new development more pressing than the groceries he'd come for, Dex tucked his phone into his pocket and headed for his pickup truck.

He could always come back for the groceries another time.

But he needed to speak with Becca immediately.

CHAPTER 3

The bed and breakfast was easy to find based on the directions Zoey had received in the email from its owner. It was located on Main Street, two doors away from a bustling restaurant with an outdoor patio. The smell of roast beef and coffee wafted out from the restaurant and filled Zoey's nostrils as she drove past in search of a parking spot.

Her stomach rumbled. She'd only munched on a slice of toast with a cup of coffee in her haste to leave New York this morning, and she'd had nothing ever since. Zoey enjoyed a hearty meal, and thankfully, it didn't show on her figure. She'd planned to grab some sandwiches from the food section at the grocery store on her way out, but that plan had obviously been thwarted. Now, she was so hungry she could eat a horse. Maybe she'd stop by the restaurant once she'd settled in.

Zoey found a public parking spot two streets over. She paid for a weekly pass, parked her rented car, grabbed her carry-on luggage, and then made her way by foot until she reached the B&B.

The quaint townhouse had a short metal fence encircling it with only a simple sign denoting what it was. Zoey stepped through the gate and walked down a paved walkway until she reached the front steps and climbed up to its entrance. She pressed the bell, noticing the installed electronic keypad, and then heard a clicking sound as the door unlocked. Zoey opened the door, stepped in, and shut it behind her.

It was as if she'd stepped into another world, leaving the chaotic noise from the street behind. Zoey would have bet some sort of soundproofing had been installed in the foyer. The cream-walled interior was much larger than she'd expected and boasted gleaming wide-plank hardwood floors, a high ceiling with exposed wood beams, and a small sitting area adjacent to a long winding staircase.

"Hello!" A young woman in a yellow summer dress with blonde hair wrapped in a bun hurried toward her. A warm smile split her face. "Welcome to

Prissy's Bed and Breakfast," she said. "How may I help you?"

"Hi, I'm Zoey. I have a room reservation starting today."

Recognition lit up in the woman's eyes, and she extended her hand to shake Zoey's. "Welcome! We've been expecting you. I'm Connie. I exchanged emails with you a few days ago."

Zoey accepted her handshake. She'd expected someone older—Connie didn't look any older than twenty. "Nice to meet you."

"Same here. And by the way I'm not the owner." Connie chuckled. "Don't worry, everyone always has the same look on their face when they meet me. Miss Prissy is my aunt, and you'll probably get to meet her later. Is this your first time in Dexin Valley?"

Zoey took an immediate liking to the young lady. "Yes. I had no idea this town existed until a friend pointed it out to me. It's very charming." Zoey had noticed the flowering meadows that stretched out for miles on either side of the road and the twinkling streams of water interspersed between them as she'd entered the town. Towering mountains in the background had completed the enchanting picture.

"It sure is. I hope you enjoy your stay here. Why

don't I check you in and then show you to your room?"

Zoey smiled. "That would be perfect."

Zoey looked around the room even as she placed her carry-on on the bed. It looked clean, cozy, and inviting with its mint, brown, and yellow color palette, the decor a mix of modern and country style furnishings.

Weathered wood graced the head of the queen-sized bed that was covered with a yellow and mint stitched quilt and plush pillows which matched the curtains. Zoey loved the distressed mint coffee table and its matching armoire, which went well with a tufted chair nestled in the corner with a floral painting hanging over it. A small wicker basket filled with fresh fruits, water, and a welcome card rested on the coffee table. But most of all, she adored the small alcove in which sat a white vintage bath tub and matching sink with antique brass hardware.

Zoey stepped out onto the adjoining balcony and found the most adorable spot to drink her early morning coffee—two wicker chairs occupied the space, a distressed stool between them. Potted plants stood in a corner, and she had a stellar view that overlooked a back garden. Zoey could hear the cooing of birds in the distance.

The room was perfect for her needs, and Zoey would have loved to just stay in and take a nap, but she needed to find some food to satiate her hunger.

She opened her luggage and pulled out some fresh clothes. A few minutes later, she'd changed out of her skirt and now wore a pair of jeans. *Much better*. She stuffed her luggage in the armoire and slung her handbag on her shoulder.

Zoey exited the room and locked it behind her, the access codes for the main entrance and her room already memorized. Then she headed down the long winding stairs and soon arrived back at the foyer.

She'd planned to ask Connie for a list of the best places to eat, but Connie was attending to another guest, so Zoey explored her surroundings while she waited.

An arched doorway on the left led to a dining area with a rustic dining table surrounded by chairs reminiscent of the type her family had when they'd lived in Texas. A filled bookcase lined one side of its wall. Zoey could also see a glimpse of the country-style kitchen that extended beyond it.

"Oh, my! I didn't know we had a pretty one

here," a pleasant voice said with a hint of a western drawl. Zoey turned to see a middle-aged lady with silvery short hair standing a few feet behind her.

"I'm Miss Prissy," the woman said with a broad smile. "Welcome to my home."

"Hello. I'm Zoey," Zoey said.

"Nice to meet you, Zoey," Miss Prissy responded.

Zoey gestured around her. "You have a beautiful home."

"Why, thank you. So, Miss Zoey, what brings you to these parts?"

To Zoey, she seemed merely curious and about as harmless as a grandmother. "I came for an interview."

"So you're a doctor?"

Zoey's eyes widened. "How did you know?"

"It's either work at the ER center or at a ranch that brings folks to these parts. And you ain't a rancher," Miss Prissy said confidently.

"Is everything alright with the room?" Connie had finished with her other guest and had come over. "Did you need anything?"

"The room is perfect," Zoey responded. "I need to grab some food, and I was wondering if you had a list of best places to eat around here."

"How about I throw in free lunch and dinner?

Delivered hot right to your room," Miss Prissy said. "In exchange for a little favor."

Favor? Zoey didn't really know these folks, and the last thing she needed was to be beholden to anyone.

"Don't worry," Miss Prissy said. She seemed to have picked up on Zoey's suspicion. "It's nothing dangerous."

"Miss Prissy is the best cook in these parts and owns the restaurant two doors away," Connie chimed in with pride.

Well, that might be true if the smell of the food from the restaurant was anything to go by. The convenience of not having to go out to look for food would be awesome too, so Zoey wondered if she should listen first to what Miss Prissy had to say. "What's the favor?"

"You go out on three blind dates."

Zoey hid her surprise. "Blind dates? How do you know I'm single?"

Miss Prissy chuckled. "Young lady, you're as pretty as a button. If you were married, your husband wouldn't let you come down here all alone." She looked down at Zoey's left hand. "And you have no ring on your finger."

Well, her logic somewhat made sense. But Zoey

wasn't keen on blind dates—she'd felt like a cow with a for-sale sign on her neck the last time she'd been on one. And then there was the issue of safety. What if the guys on these dates were dangerous?

"My matchmaking business does a really good job of checking out the men's backgrounds and vetting them. These are men that would make great matches. You have nothing to fear," Miss Prissy reassured her as if she'd read her thoughts. "Most of them I've seen grow up in this town. They're as gentlemanly as they come."

"True," Connie chimed in.

"You know them?" Zoey asked.

"I grew up with them and know their families. They are good people," Connie said.

Okay, maybe the dates wouldn't be so bad and could make her trip more entertaining and memorable. But she had to make clear her stance on relationships. "I'm not looking for a relationship or a husband."

"That's fine too," Miss Prissy said. "I'd love a testimonial of your experience on the dates instead. Even though we'd love the couples we match up in our business to fall in love and get married, we'd also like our service to appeal to the few who are just looking for safe dates at first."

"Where would these dates take place?"

"The first would be in my restaurant," Miss Prissy said. "Lots of folks around, so nothing to worry about. The other two could be in places of your choosing."

Zoey thought for a moment. Three blind dates in exchange for free lunches and dinners throughout her stay with the right to determine the venue? This seemed like a no-brainer. She'd already planned to explore the town when she could. Maybe this was a good way to do it with company. "Okay, I accept as long as the men realize it's only a date and nothing more."

"Perfect." Miss Prissy rubbed her hands together. "This is going to be so much fun! I'll drop off the details later. Right now, we need to get you fed. Connie, could you bring some of the food to the dining table?"

"Yes, ma'am," Connie replied.

Miss Prissy linked her arm with Zoey. "Now let's sit over there, and you tell me all about yourself."

Zoey allowed herself to be led to the dining area.

But she prayed she wasn't making a mistake.

CHAPTER 4

Dex marched into Dexin Ranch's main house where Max, Becca, their daughter, Chloe, and Maggie—until recently—lived. Dex and his younger brother, Jax, had their own properties on the ranch, though they came to the main house for meal times with the rest of the family.

Dexin Ranch was a small ranch operation—compared to others in the valley—that raised show horses and cattle. Dex and his brothers ran the ranch, though Max was also a professor of emergency medicine at Dexington Medical Center and was now the new director of the soon-to-be-opened Dexin ER Center.

The rustic log-and-stone living area was empty, no Becca or Chloe to be seen. The house was unusually quiet, which meant either they were in their living space in Max's section of the house or they were in Becca's home office. Dex headed toward the office to search for them there first.

He stepped through the double French doors on the right and soon reached the entrance to the office. Dex knocked once, and then twice, but there was no response. Then he turned the doorknob and opened the door softly.

The large space was decorated in all-white with pops of pale blue and gold furnishings, and was divided into a work area for Becca with her own chair, desk, and computer, an area for client consultations with a white tufted couch and matching gold herringbone chairs around a coffee table, a play area for Chloe that featured a miniature version of her mom's desk and chair, and enough storage solutions to keep the office organized.

Becca—a striking woman in her early forties with dark brown hair—had her head down on her desk. Chloe lay on the sofa all curled up into herself.

Becca looked up as he entered, her green eyes bleary with sleep. "Hey, Dex." She stifled a yawn.

"Hi, Becca. I tried your number a couple of times, but it rang through," Dex said.

"Sorry. I don't know when I fell asleep. Just had a

ton of work to get through." She ran a hand through her hair. "What's going on?"

"I need to talk to you," he said quietly.

"Alright. Let's go outside so we don't wake Chloe. I'm not yet ready for her tornado." She got up from the desk and came around toward the door.

Dex held the door open for her until she passed through and then he shut it quietly. Becca led the way until they were back in the living room. She turned to Dex. "What's going on? You seem bothered, like you have a bee in your bonnet."

"Did you sign me up for Miss Prissy's match-making business?" He waved the newspaper he'd bought from the newsstand on his way back in front of her.

Becca accepted the newspaper and scanned it. Her lips widened into a smile, and her green eyes sparkled. "You look great, Dex," she said.

"That's not the point, Becca. You never told me about it. You never asked for my permission."

"I didn't?"

"No."

"That's odd. I'm so sorry, Dex," she said in an apologetic tone. "I thought I did." She rubbed her forehead. "What's going on with me lately?"

"What do you mean?"

"I've been forgetting things." She slumped onto the large couch in the center of the living area. "And I've been feeling so tired lately, like a truck ran over me."

An overwhelming sense of dread washed over Dex. He hoped nothing was wrong with Becca. They'd almost lost Becca and Max a few months ago when an arsonist set the horse barn on fire. Thankfully, no one, including the horses, had been hurt. Chloe finally had her parents together after so many years. The family couldn't afford anything happening to Becca again. "You should see a doctor."

"I know. I already booked an appointment for Monday."

This was serious if Becca had already scheduled one. Dex sent up a quick prayer for protection and healing. He took a seat beside her. "Don't worry. I'm sure everything will be fine."

"I pray so. For now, could you not tell Max? He already has a lot on his plate, and I don't want him getting all worried, especially if it ends up being nothing. You know how he can get."

Dex knew indeed. Max would want to run every test on earth to make sure Becca was alright. Dex had been a victim of this more times than he could count.

"Okay. But you have to promise to tell him about it as soon as you get back from the appointment."

"I promise."

"Good. I'll get Jax to watch Chloe on Monday."

"Thank you. Again, I'm sorry about the matchmaking business. But could you just go with it since it's already out there? I do think it's a great idea. Dex, you know you need to meet a girl before you can marry her."

"I have my own ways."

"I'm sure you do, but a little help never hurts."

Dex didn't agree with her, but he'd already assented to it. It was just as well—she already had enough on her plate to handle and didn't need to be distracted by this as well. Besides, backing out at this point would only give his family a bad name, something he would never allow to happen.

A playful ringtone split the air. Becca pulled out her phone from her jean pocket and checked the screen. "It's Miss Prissy." She answered the call. "Hello." Becca listened for a few minutes and then said: "Okay. Thanks." Then she ended the call.

"What was that all about?" Dex asked.

"She just called to say that the first blind date has been scheduled."

Dex's heart quickened. "Already? I just saw her a few minutes ago!"

"You know Miss Prissy. She moves fast."

"When?"

"Tomorrow night."

"That's too soon!"

"I know. But isn't it better to get it over and done with?"

Becca had a point, even though it was clear she was saying so to make sure he didn't bail out. Yes, it was probably best to take care of it as soon as possible so that he could get on with his life.

Dex only hoped it would be a painless experience.

CHAPTER 5

*D*ex headed into his house on a separate section of the ranch after locking his pick-up truck. Though a single-level home, its exterior shared similar features with the main house, but it boasted a large front garden Dex loved to tend to. The interior was also different—he'd used the more masculine colors of grey, dark blue, and brown with a splash of teal, though the occasional Chloe toy in bright neon colors always managed to find its way in.

Sunday church had been more boisterous than usual. Dex had planned to slip in and out in stealth mode, but the parishioners had had other ideas. He'd been swamped with folks shaking his hands and wishing him luck. Even the pastor had slapped his back and bid him success. It seemed Miss Prissy had done a thorough job of announcing the details of his date to the whole town.

Dex had gritted his teeth and bore through it with a smile on his face. He hated the attention, but there was nothing he could do about it at this point. But now that he was back home in his natural habitat, he was already exhausted just thinking about the upcoming date.

But one question crossed his mind above the others: what kind of lady was she? He'd called Miss Prissy to find out, but she'd insisted it would be a surprise, one he'd like. Dex had no choice but to believe her.

He'd chosen to miss lunch at the main house today to avoid questions from Max, Becca, and Chloe about the date. Instead, Dex headed toward his gourmet kitchen that featured dark blue cabinets, a large quartz island and a light backsplash.

The house was designed with an open floor plan layout and had top-of-the-line stainless steel appliances, including a commercial-grade gas range, a double oven, and a French door refrigerator. A walk-in pantry made it easy for him to reach his vast spice collection, staple ingredients, and fine olive oils. Dex enjoyed cooking and made sure he had all he needed for his numerous experiments.

Some of them made their way to the main house, while others were shared with the employees on the ranch.

Dex pulled open his warming drawer and lifted out the dish of cowboy lasagna he'd made early this morning before church. It was chock-full of ground beef, sausage, mushrooms, and some vegetables— Dex didn't care for pepperoni, so he'd left it out. He grabbed a fork, settled on one of the stools around the island, and dug in.

Fifteen minutes later, he was done and had even washed the dishes. Now he had nothing else to do but to prep for the date.

Dex headed into his master bedroom. What was he going to wear? He was a laid-back kind of guy and typically wore jeans and shirts. Maybe it was best the lady saw him how he usually was, instead of dressing differently and setting an unrealistic expectation in her mind.

He entered his walk-in closet and looked through his vast array of shirts and jeans. Everything looked great, but nothing called to him.

He rubbed his forehead. This was too much work. Dex would typically pull out the nearest available clothes on any given day, and now the mental analysis of deciding what to wear was hurting his brain. Yet his family and Miss Prissy would expect him to at least make the effort.

Dex let out a sigh and stepped out of the closet. What was he going to do?

His door jerked open. He glanced in its direction, only to see Jax, his younger brother, step in. Jax looked more like Dex in his facial features and height than his twin, Rex. Jax was the extroverted one in the family and the financial brain behind the ranch. He made sure all the numbers worked, handled payroll, and even made investments on its behalf. Yet, he was still put to task on the ranch whenever he was needed.

"Hey, why didn't you knock?" Dex said.

Jax gave him a funny look. "I've never knocked on your door, and it has never bothered you before." He plopped down on the custom-sized large bed in the room. "What's going on?"

Dex leaned against the wall. "It's this date thing."

Jax grinned. "You're like a celebrity now."

Dex groaned. "Oh, don't add to it. I already got a bellyful of it at church."

"Does Chloe know?"

"Is there anything she doesn't?" The five-year-old had an opinion for everything. "I'm sure Max and Becca are having a hard time stopping her from coming here."

"I can imagine her jumping up and down on this bed while giving you her valued advice."

Dex grimaced. "Yikes! No thanks. I know she means well, but I might end up on the date with pink socks."

Jax raised an eyebrow. "You have those?"

"I'm sure she'll bring some. Max complained he'd had to wear a bunch of them to work for the past two weeks to please her. She'll decide that I'm fair game too. And you know how she pulls out those waterworks if we deny her."

Jax nodded. He'd been at the receiving end of Chloe's world famous waterworks one too many times. "But seriously, you want to settle down, right?"

"Yes, but not like this. I like to do things privately. This just puts too much unnecessary pressure on both parties. It's already awkward enough as it is meeting someone on a blind date. Now I feel like I'm the clown in a circus show that's about to begin."

Jax brushed his blonde hair away from his forehead. "I'm sure it will work out fine. The Lord works in mysterious ways. If it doesn't, then it's just another experience."

"Not you too."

"Dex, just go with the flow."

Dex let out another sigh. "Alright."

"So what are you wearing?"

Dex pinched the bridge of his nose. "That's part of the problem. I can't seem to decide. I'll probably just end up wearing one of my regulars."

"I knew you would say that." Jax jumped to his feet. "I'll be right back." He stepped out of the room and soon returned with a shopping bag in tow. He extended it to Dex. "Open it."

Dex accepted the bag and pulled out a beautiful teal and dark blue plaid shirt and a custom pair of high-end boots. Dex had a thing for boots and had tried to snag this brand before, but it was always sold out. "How did you get these?" he said, indicating the boots.

"I called a friend who called a friend that works at that shop. I know you've always wanted a pair of these, though I think the ones you make are much nicer."

"But look at this stitching and the design on the inside—"

Jax held up his hand. "Why don't we focus on the date for now?"

Dex chuckled. "Okay. Thanks, Jax."

"You're welcome. I know you want to stay in

your style, but you need to dress up for the little lady."

"Little lady?"

"Sure. She's the woman you're getting married to." Jax flashed him a wicked grin. "You can't be thinking that with all the hoopla in town that you'll just finish the date and that will be it?"

Dex grabbed a pillow and threw it at his head. "Get out. I was already wondering when you'd start with all your nonsense."

Jax dodged it, laughing as the pillow landed on the floor. "I'm going, I'm going. A man can't even be appreciated for two seconds. Good luck, stud buddy." He hurried out and slammed the door before Dex could throw another pillow at him.

Dex picked up the fallen pillow and dropped it back on the bed. Thanks to Jax, his what-to-wear dilemma was solved.

Now he prayed the actual date wouldn't be a disaster.

CHAPTER 6

oey entered the restaurant and looked around. The place was teeming with people, most sitting at tables with hardly a spare seat —not exactly what she'd expected on a Sunday night. Her eyes began to scan the restaurant, searching for the clue Miss Prissy had told her to look for.

"Good evening, ma'am," a voice said. Zoey looked up to see a stocky waiter in an apron over a white shirt and black pants standing in front of her. "Welcome to Miss Prissy's Restaurant," he said. "Would you like a table?"

"No, thank you. I'm meeting someone here." Her eyes had spotted the vase of red roses in a table set apart toward the back. *Bingo!* There was a man already seated there with his head bent as if reading something. His profile looked familiar, though she couldn't see his face. A cowboy hat rested on the seat beside him.

"Let me know if you need anything else," the waiter said.

"I will. Thank you."

Zoey adjusted the strap of her bag and held it close to the front of her dress as she made her way to the table. She'd risked another departure from her usual attire and had donned a yellow and black long-sleeved floral midi dress that seemed to go nicely with her wedge heels. She'd let down her hair, and it now hung in waves around her face.

Soon she reached the table, and the man looked up from his phone as she approached.

Zoey froze, and shock rippled through her. It was the same guy from the grocery store!

Her ears turned red. Why did it have to be him of all people? Now she would be wondering every minute of the date if he remembered her embarrassing moment.

The man rose to his feet. His eyes widened with recognition, but he made no mention of the incident. "Good evening, ma'am."

If he could ignore it, she could do the same. "Hi, I'm Zoey," she said.

"I'm Dex. Nice to meet you." He moved over and pulled out her chair for her.

Zoey sat down and waited for him to return to his seat. Now she had a better view of him, and she had to admit he was one fine specimen: broad shoulders that filled out his shirt and a chiseled jawline that could cut glass. His plaid shirt brought out the different shades of brown in his eyes and did nothing to hide his well-toned frame. She could tell it wasn't from working out at the gym—this body type could only be from hard old-fashioned labor. A man who worked with his hands. One point in his favor—Zoey couldn't stand guys who were all talk and no action. This was a man's man, yet there was a softness about him that called out to her.

"So have you been here for a while?" Zoey asked.

He shook his head. "Just arrived a few minutes ago," he responded in that western drawl that wreaked havoc to her insides.

She swallowed. "I see you were keeping yourself busy in the meantime." Zoey gestured at his phone.

"Just watching some videos," he responded.

"Anything interesting?"

"I'm not sure you'd like these."

"Try me." Zoey usually had a hard time keeping

the conversation going during blind dates, but something about Dex seemed to have loosened her tongue.

"Okay." He unlocked the screen and passed his phone to her. Zoey accepted it and studied the screen. The video seemed to be of some sort of leather craft workshop.

Interesting. "Do you work with leather?" she asked, handing the phone back to him.

"I do. It's a hobby." Zoey expected him to elaborate more, but he said nothing else.

"Hello," an unfamiliar voice said.

Zoey looked up to see a middle-aged couple standing beside their table. Dex got to his feet. "Hello, ma'am, sir."

"Hi, Dex," the matronly woman said. "Date going on well?" she asked.

Zoey's face warmed. How had the woman known she was on a date? Had Dex told her? Zoey could see the woman peering curiously at her.

"Hmmm." Dex didn't say anything else.

"Alright, we'll leave you to it. Have a wonderful evening," the woman said.

"You too, ma'am," he said. The couple walked away, and Dex sat back down.

That was weird. If the couple knew they were on a date, why had they bothered to interrupt them?

"Did you tell them we were on a date?" Zoey asked.

Dex glanced at her sharply. "No. Would you like something to drink?" he asked instead.

"Yes, please. I'd like some ginger ale."

"Coming right up." He hailed a waiter who was walking by. The waiter took their drink orders and then left.

Zoey leaned back on her chair. "So what do you do, Dex?"

"I run a ranch with my brothers."

So he had brothers. Did they all look alike? But she couldn't ask. She had no idea how he would react to the question.

"What about you?" he asked.

"I'm a doctor."

He didn't look surprised. "You're not from these parts, right?"

"I'm from New York. Just here on vacation."

"And you signed up for a blind date?"

She straightened her shoulders. What was he implying? "No law against that."

"Hi, Dex," another voice said. This time it was an elderly woman in her sixties.

He rose to his feet again. "Good evening, ma'am," he said.

"Enjoying your date?" she asked. It was like they'd scripted these interruptions. Who were all these people, and how did they know about the date?

"I'm good," Dex said.

"Say hello to Maggie for me when she gets back," the elderly lady said.

Maggie? Who was Maggie? Some girlfriend? If that was the case, why was he even here on a date?

"I will," Dex responded.

"Alright. I'll leave you to it." She made her way toward the restaurant's exit where a younger man seemed to be waiting for her.

"Maggie is my foster mom," Dex explained.

"You live with your mom?"

"Sort of."

Yikes. She was on a date with a momma's boy. That was a big fat "no" on her list. *Check please!* And what was it with all these 'drive-by' greetings? Couldn't a girl just finish a date in peace?

Their drinks arrived, and Zoey took a sip of the cold drink.

"Would you like to order now?" the waiter asked.

Dex looked at Zoey for confirmation. She nodded. "Sure," he replied.

The waiter handed them each a menu.

"Zoey, what would you like?" Dex asked.

Zoey glanced at the list. Most of the menu items had too many calories for her to consume at this time of the day, though they looked delicious. She opted for some smoky BBQ baked beans with a side of cornbread. Dex placed their orders, and the waiter left.

"So, Dr. Zoey, tell me a little bit about yourself," Dex said.

"Hello, Dex." This time it was a man in his early forties with a mustache he kept twirling.

Oh, not again! Had their table been designated a central train station without her knowledge?

"Hello, Jeff," Dex responded.

Jeff slapped him on the back. "You enjoying yourself?"

Well, we would be if you folks weren't interrupting every thirty seconds, Zoey thought.

"Hmmm," Dex responded. He didn't seemed fazed by what was happening.

"Alright, enjoy the rest of your night. Goodnight, ma'am." Jeff tipped his hat at Zoey. She nodded in response. Then he walked away.

"Dex, is there something about this date I should know about?"

"What do you mean?"

"People keep dropping by to say hello. I don't see them doing the same to other patrons."

Dex twirled the drink in his hand. "You didn't know?" He placed the glass back on the table.

"Know what?"

"That the news of our date was probably leaked by the organizers. And there's a high likelihood that most of the folks in the restaurant are probably here to watch the date."

"What?" she exclaimed a bit more loudly than usual. Zoey could hear the room grow silent as the other patrons turned their attention to her table. Was this some sort of reality TV show she hadn't known about?

She could feel her face growing warm. Now she couldn't even utter a word without the whole restaurant listening in on their conversation!

Zoey jumped to her feet. "I need to use the bathroom," she said. "I'll be right back." Hopefully, by then, the patrons would have turned back to their own discussions or she would have come up with a solution. Zoey made a note to herself to never schedule a date in a restaurant except in a private room.

She slung the strap of her bag over her shoulder and began to head in the direction she suspected the bathrooms would be.

Something crashed on the table. Zoey jumped back only to see that her bag had knocked down Dex's drink. The orange mango mocktail had spilled on the table and found its way down Dex's side and onto his clothes.

Oh no! "I'm so sorry," Zoey said. She grabbed her napkin and began to dab at his stained clothes.

He stayed her hand. "I can do it." He took his napkin and started wiping down his shirt.

"I'm really sorry."

"It's fine," he said as he continued dabbing his shirt.

By now, Zoey could feel the eyes of the other patrons in the restaurant boring into her. *Ugh.* What was it about this guy and her and embarrassing situations? This blind date was a disaster, and she needed to end it soon before something worse happened. "I have to go," she said.

Dex stared at her for a moment. "Okay," he finally said.

Zoey felt her heart sink a little. He'd given up so easily? Sure, she'd been the one to request to end the date, but she'd expected a little protest. Had the date been that bad for him? Did he hate being here with her? "Cool. It was nice meeting you, Dex. Have a wonderful night."

"Let me walk you to your car," he said.

"No need." He wanted nothing to do with her, so there was no point in him seeing her off. He hadn't even bothered to ask for her number. Besides, she was only going two doors away.

"What about—"

"Goodnight." Zoey walked away before he had a chance to say anything else.

She'd dolled up for nothing. Instead, she'd ended up with an empty stomach and a bruised ego. Miss Prissy's promised dinner would help with the first, but she wasn't sure how to fix the latter.

The restaurant remained silent even as she strode through. It felt like she was taking a walk of shame. But Zoey held her head high through it. She'd done nothing wrong.

But she'd been right about blind dates, and she wanted nothing to do with them again, especially with a certain man with warm brown eyes.

She only needed to focus on her upcoming interview tomorrow, which was what had brought her to this town in the first place.

Even though her heart still smarted from Dex's rejection.

CHAPTER 7

*D*ex drove his red pickup truck up the driveway and parked in front of his house, but he made no move to get out. Instead, he leaned back against the headrest.

The blind date had surely been a strange one. He'd thought they would have had some privacy given the location of the table, but the town, in their effort to be encouraging, had disrupted the date. The drink disaster must have been the final straw for Zoey. Dex didn't blame her for leaving immediately.

Zoey had looked more beautiful than she had at the grocery store—he'd noticed the other men at the restaurant couldn't stop staring at her. Her scent had been soft and subtle, and he'd felt it wrap around him as she'd settled into the chair opposite him. But she'd been the last person he'd expected to meet on the date, even though a part of him had been pleased to see her again. How had Miss Prissy roped her in, and what had made her agree to it? This was one mystery he wasn't going to be able to figure out.

It had been interesting to find out she was a doctor. For a minute, he'd hoped she was here to work at the ER center, but it'd turned out she was only here on a vacation. Not that he'd developed a crush on her or anything—it would have just been nice to get to know her better. He'd been tongue-tied for a bit, unlike his usual confident self, and that might have turned her off. He'd wanted to suggest that she wait and get her meal packed up as takeout. Instead, she'd cut him off. Maybe she'd wanted to get away from him as fast as possible.

Dex let out a long sigh. Well, it was over and done with. He'd tried the blind date route, and it had failed. It was best to put everything behind him and concentrate on the mentee spot he was hoping to snag.

He opened the door of his truck and jumped down. The night air was surprisingly cool, which he appreciated. It would make for a much easier sleep tonight. Dex locked the truck and headed to the front door. The small stoop was dark, and he guessed the light was busted. He'd fix it tomorrow—he was too tired tonight to take care of it.

"Hello, Dex."

Dex jumped back in fright. "What the—"

"It's just me, Becca." She stepped out of the dark area until he could see her face.

"Hey, you frightened me," Dex said.

"Sorry."

"What are you doing here?"

"I heard about what happened at the restaurant."

Dex ran his hand through his hair. This was ridiculous. So who in this town hadn't heard about the outcome of the date? As a man—as much as he hated the invasion of his privacy—he could deal with it. But how would Zoey handle the extra attention, especially since she was a stranger to these parts?

"I'm sorry," Becca said. "I was the one who signed you up for this. I never expected it would fail."

"It's not your fault," Dex said. "You should really be home with Chloe."

"I needed the fresh air. It tends to reinvigorate me."

Dex forgot about the date, his concern for Becca's health rising to the forefront instead. "Are you still tired most of the time?"

Becca nodded. "But the mystery of what's going on will be all over tomorrow once I see the doctor."

"How are you getting there? Are you taking the helicopter?" The ranch had a helipad on the property.

Becca shook her head. "I don't really feel like riding it. Max is going up to Dexington after his early morning interview, and he'll drop me off at Leah's place." Leah was Becca's older sister who ran a well-known lingerie company in Dexington—the town where Becca had grown up and where her doctor was based.

Interview? "We have a new doctor coming?"

"It seems so, but I don't really know much about the candidate. Max seems to like whoever he or she is. Anyway, Max will need to return here before I'm done in Dexington, so Leah's chauffeur will bring me back."

"I pray everything goes well at the appointment."

"Me too." She yawned. "I guess it's time to head back."

"Let me drop you off."

Becca shook her head. "It's not a big deal, and the walk will do me good."

"Are you sure? I can walk back with you if you like."

"Positive. I need the time to clear my head, and

it's a short walk. Max will probably be wrangling Chloe into bed by now."

Dex chuckled. "I can imagine how that's going."

Becca laughed. "That's why I snuck out. But it's time I went to save him." She gave him a quick hug. "I'll see you later. I'm sure you'll meet the woman for you soon."

"Good night, Becca."

She waved over her head at him as she walked away. Despite what she'd said, Dex followed her a few feet behind until he could see the main house and then watched her enter it.

Then he turned and headed back to his home.

The blind date was over with, and what had happened tonight would probably blow over in a few days when the town found a new topic to gossip about.

But why did a part of him wish he could see her again?

CHAPTER 8

Zoey parked her vehicle—which seemed dwarfed by everything around it—in front of the sprawling log-and-stone house and got out. It'd been too many years since she'd been at a ranch, yet she'd never seen one as well-kept and picturesque as this.

She'd been wowed by the view as she'd driven through the massive wrought-iron gates and up a driveway lined by manicured flower hedges, with the meadows and majestic mountains in the far distance. She took a deep breath, and the vibrant scent of wild-flowers, the sweet smell of hay, and the refreshing early morning air filled her nostrils. If only she'd get a chance to live in a place like this. In that moment, Zoey didn't miss New York one bit.

Feeling confident in her light blue button-down shirt tucked into grey slacks, Zoey was all set for the interview. She grabbed her satchel from the front seat, locked the car, and made her way to the the entrance to the home—a massive oak door. Zoey pressed the bell, hearing the chime echoing on the other side of the door.

"I'll be right there," a warm, cultured voice said.

Zoey jumped. She hadn't expected a security camera at the door. Her eyes searched the area, but she couldn't find its location.

Then the door swung open, and a woman who could have passed for a celebrity in her cream silk blouse tucked into a pair of dark skinny jeans and a pair of oversized glasses over stunning green eyes stood in front of her. "Hello!" she said in a bright voice. "You must be Dr. Brown. I'm Becca. Welcome to Dexin Ranch." She had none of the western drawl Zoey had come to expect from the folks in this town, but she was just as warm as any of them.

"Good morning, Becca. It's nice to meet you."

Becca opened the door wider. "Come on in. My husband Max has been expecting you." So she was the wife of the director of the ER center, with whom she'd come to meet.

Zoey stepped into the home, and her eyes

widened. Of course, she'd expected the house's interior to be stunning, but this was exquisite. Logs and stones were interwoven in a genius construction to give off both a rustic and modern feel. A long, winding staircase led to a second floor. It was warm, inviting, and breathtaking. She couldn't imagine how the occupants would ever want to leave this place.

"It's beautiful, isn't it?" Becca said.

"Yes, it is," Zoey said.

"I felt the same way when I first came here." At Zoey's surprised glance: "Max's mother built this space with the help of Max and his brothers."

"It's really inviting," Zoey said as she continued to look around. The log-hewn winding staircase was a focal point she couldn't miss.

"I'm glad you like it, Dr. Brown."

Zoey turned back to her. "Please call me Zoey."

Becca smiled at her. "Please have a seat." She gestured at the large sofa in the living area. "Max is on a call and will be with you shortly."

"Thank you." Zoey settled into the couch, while Becca took the love seat opposite her.

"Would you like anything to drink?" Becca asked. "We have coffee, tea, cold lemonade, strawberry fluffy—"

"Strawberry fluffy?" Zoey couldn't help interrupting. What was that?

Becca laughed, the rich sound so carefree and inviting. Zoey was liking this intriguing woman more and more. "It's the name my daughter Chloe coined for the mint strawberry drink her grandma created for her. And here she comes."

A ball of whirlwind raced into the room and landed on Becca's lap. "Mommy, can I …Oh." It seemed she'd just noticed Zoey. "Hello."

"Zoey, meet Chloe, my wonderful daughter and queen of this home."

A pair of large, intelligent blue eyes in an angelic face framed by dark red hair stared back at her. "Nice to meet you, Chloe," Zoey said.

Those eyes studied her for a moment. "Can we keep her?" she finally said to her mom.

Zoey couldn't help laughing. She could already tell Chloe was a riot and fun to be with.

Becca's face turned pink. "I'm sorry," she said to Zoey. "Sometimes we never know what Chloe will say."

Zoey hurried to reassure her. "It's fine. She's adorable."

"Thank you." Then Becca turned to Chloe. "Zoey

is here for an interview with your father. We can't keep her, okay?"

Chloe's face fell. "Okay."

Zoey knew the child had only meant well. "But I could play with you later if you like, Chloe."

Chloe's face brightened. "Okay."

Zoey smiled at the change in her countenance. She'd always liked kids, but she'd need a relationship to have kids, and, well ….

"Hello, Dr. Brown. I'm Max Dexin. Sorry to keep you waiting." A tall bespectacled man in a white button-down shirt and grey slacks, who looked like he might have walked off the pages of a GQ magazine, strode into view. His features looked somewhat familiar, though Zoey couldn't place him.

"Daddy!" Chloe jumped up from her mom's lap and ran into her father's arms.

"I hope you've been staying out of trouble," Dr. Dexin said as he tweaked her nose.

Chloe giggled. "I tried, although Ornie wanted to follow me to my room."

"What did we say about baby goats, sweetheart?"

"They are not allowed inside the house. I left him outside, but he kept crying."

"Where's Ornie now?"

"In his house."

"Good girl. Now, Daddy has a meeting with this wonderful doctor here, so make sure you stay with Mommy, okay?"

"Okay." Dr. Dexin gave her a kiss on her cheek and then placed her down on her feet. Chloe hurried back to sit beside her mom. His piercing blue eyes then turned to Zoey. She could see where Chloe had gotten hers. "Dr. Brown, why don't we go and chat in my office?" he said.

Zoey rose to her feet. "Sounds good."

Zoey followed Dr. Dexin as he made his way past the double French doors and down the hallway to his office. This area of the house had a more modern feel with its hardwood floors and motion-activated recessed lighting.

"Hope you had an easy time finding the ranch?" he asked.

"Yes, I did," Zoey said. "The directions you sent were very helpful."

"That's great to hear. Here we are." Dr. Dexin opened a large door to the left and motioned for Zoey to enter first. Then he closed the door behind them.

Zoey could tell Dr. Dexin was an avid reader with

the extensive floor-to-ceiling bookshelves that lined the walls. She studied the book spines—some appeared to be first editions. A section was dedicated to medical books, most of which she recognized, having used the same. A large oak desk and a custom two-toned swivel chair occupied the space closest to the windows, while a large black leather sofa rested against one wall.

"You may sit," Dr. Dexin said, motioning to one of the tufted visitors' chairs that faced the desk. He moved behind it and sat in the swivel chair.

Zoey settled in and waited to hear what Dr. Dexin had to say.

"Welcome to Dexin Valley, Dr. Brown. I hope your trip down here from New York was safe."

"Yes, it was," Zoey replied. "This area is beautiful."

"It sure is," Dr. Dexin said with pride. "But we've never had enough medical resources to serve the needs of this community, which was why my family and I decided to open the ER center."

Zoey gave him a surprised look. "It wasn't a decision by the town?"

"Of course, we got the approval of the town with the zoning laws and all, but it's been my family's dream for a long time to establish a hospital in the valley, and now it's almost a reality."

A knock sounded on the door, and Becca entered. She set a glass of what looked like cool strawberry drink in front of Zoey. "It's strawberry fluffy," she said. "You'll love it."

Zoey smiled at her. "Thank you."

"Thanks, Becca," Dr. Dexin said.

"Anytime, love." She winked at him, and Dr. Dexin's lips turned up into a smile. From the love shining in his eyes, it was clear he adored Becca. "I'll be in the living room if you need me." She stepped out and closed the door behind her.

"It's been more than three months, and I still can't believe this wonderful woman is my wife," Dr. Dexin said.

Three months? Didn't they have a five-year-old daughter?

"Becca and I got married five years ago, but didn't know it." At Zoey's disbelieving look: "I know it's hard to believe. A story for another day. Then we reconnected a couple months ago, and that's when I found out I had a daughter. Even though they've only been in my life for a short time, they mean the world to me. Are you married, Dr. Brown?"

"No, I'm not."

"If you get the chance, it's absolutely worth it with the right person." He leaned back in his chair. "I'm sorry. I'm rambling."

Zoey chuckled. "It's okay."

"So, back to the reason we decided to open the center. Dexin Valley and its environs, beyond the town you've seen, are filled with ranches, which are all spread out. With the nearest medical facilities almost two hours away, we've had our set of challenges getting adequate medical care over the years. So, we decided it was high time we had our own emergency services, staffed with the best doctors and state-of-the-art equipment, that would rival some of the leading centers on the east coast.

"We got the permits and licenses we needed, put all the funds in place, and reached out to the Dexington Healthcare Board to see if they were interested in collaborating with us. Dexington Medical could send their residents to us for a one-month ER residency rotation in exchange for our ER center providing support services, including our helicopter airlift services, to them. Also, we agreed to pay the residents ourselves during their one-month rotation here."

"That's a lot of investment."

Dr. Dexin smiled. "Money isn't a concern for us."

This family had to be super rich if that was the case. From the somewhat moderate lifestyle she'd seen, Zoey liked that they didn't flaunt their wealth.

Dr. Dexin took a sip from the glass of water that had been on his desk before continuing. "Right now, we're setting up all the equipment, which shouldn't take more than a month to accomplish," Dr. Dexin said. "Then we'll have the center open shortly thereafter. That's why we've started interviewing candidates for all the necessary positions. Of course, some of our colleagues had already indicated their interest a few months ago, but we've kept some spots available to fill now. Any questions so far?"

"It sounds interesting. But are you bringing in a lot of experienced staff?" Zoey took a sip of the strawberry drink as she waited for him to respond. It was indeed fluffy but not too sweet. Just her kind of drink. Maybe she'd ask Becca for the recipe before she left.

"Yes, we are," Dr. Dexin replied. "Enough experienced attendings, nurses, and other medical staff in Emergency Medicine, ICU, General Surgery, Pediatrics, Ob-Gyn, and Radiology. I, an ER attending, and my foster mom's husband, Dr. Peter Taylor, a well-known New York general surgeon, will be running the center as well, so we're bringing a lot of experience on board just by ourselves."

Dr. Peter Taylor? Wasn't he one of the most sought-after surgeons in New York? Zoey had even heard he'd received an excellence award in recent times. Wow, Dr. Dexin meant it when he said he was bringing in some serious talent, which eased some of Zoey's concerns about being able to grow her skills in this out-of-the-way facility.

"The beauty of this center is that we'll get to go really deep in Emergency Care and be more specialized than a typical trauma center would be. Each EM subspecialty would get the chance to broaden its scope of services offered to patients while still engaging in extensive cutting-edge research," Dr. Dexin continued. "We hope to be more nimble and flexible in experimenting with and adapting new emergency care approaches, without being limited by the typical bureaucratic structure. We plan to grow it to become a model center like no other."

This was great to hear. Zoey could get behind something like this, assuming they could execute it well.

"Finally, we'll also be accepting a few newly minted attendings, which, from what I understand

and from looking at your credentials and recommendations, you are."

"Yes, I am," Zoey replied.

"I'm assuming you've received a lot of offers already."

"I have."

"So why would you be interested in working here at the ER Center?"

"I've always appreciated a little slower pace of life. I grew up in Texas, even though I've lived in New York for many years."

"Interesting. So you've been on a ranch before?"

"I have, but that was many years ago when I was much younger."

"If you're looking for a good quality of life, Dexin Valley is where you need to be."

Zoey gave him a brief smile. That seemed true, but there were a lot of factors she still had to consider before making up her mind. Even though relationships were off the table for her now, at some point, she would like to settle down, and she didn't want to limit her options. She hadn't seen as many young people around town as she would have liked. Even the one blind date she'd gone on had been a failure.

"Do you have any more questions for me?" Dr. Dexin asked.

"Would the attendings have hospital rights at Dexington Medical? Just wondering if there would be opportunities for collaborations with some of the doctors there."

Dr. Dexin nodded. "Yes, you would." He leaned back. "Now here's what I think will happen once we're up and running: I'm guessing some of the doctors at Dexington, especially those with young families, will choose to move down here. The air is fresher, and the environment is great for children. This will further push up the real estate value, such that those who settle here first would have the best chance at snagging good deals. I know you said you aren't married yet, but you never know what the good Lord has in mind. We could also end up with more ER doctors in this area than you would imagine."

"Glad to hear it. I have no further questions."

"Great. We'll get back to you in the next forty-eight hours. If offered a spot, you'll be given a short turnaround time to make a final decision. You can make counteroffers within that time frame, but our final offer will be made at the end of that period. We need to make sure we have enough time to bring in a replacement for the center's opening if an offer is made to you and you choose to decline it."

Zoey's eyes widened. The process was a lot faster

than she'd experienced with other hospitals, but it would be interesting to see how it played out. "Sounds good to me."

"It was great meeting you, Dr. Brown." Dr. Dexin rose and extended his hand to her. "I wish you good luck with everything."

Zoey got to her feet and accepted his handshake. "It was wonderful meeting you too, Dr. Dexin." She released his hand.

"You can call me Max, now that the interview is over. We're a bit informal around here."

"Then you can call me Zoey."

"Zoey it is." He looked at his watch. "I need to start heading down to Dexington if I want to make my meeting."

"I'll be on my way then."

The door jerked open at that moment, and Becca burst into the office, her face a mask of concern. "Max, we need your help."

"What is it?" Max said. He'd already started coming around the desk.

"It's Dex. He's hurt."

CHAPTER 9

Zoey's eyes widened. Dex? The same Dex she'd had a blind date with? The name was uncommon enough, and the town was small enough, that it had to be the same one. She looked back at Max, and then it dawned on her. Now she could see the resemblance between Dex and him. No wonder he'd looked familiar! But why hadn't Dex revealed his relationship to Dr. Dexin when Zoey had mentioned she was a doctor?

Yet that wasn't what was most important now. A man had been hurt, and she was a doctor first of all, no matter what had happened between them. It was only right she made sure he was okay.

"Give me one moment," Max said to Zoey as he headed toward the door. "I'll be right back."

"I'll come with you," Zoey replied.

"Okay." He hurried out after Becca, and Zoey followed suit.

They arrived back at the living room with Zoey right behind Max. Dex was settled on the couch with his left leg on the coffee table.

Zoey's pulse raced from seeing him, but she forced herself to ignore it. All she had to do was make sure he was alright, and then she'd leave, right?

"Woah! What's that on your leg?" Max asked as he pointed to the gigantic swath of bandage around Dex's ankle.

"That's Becca's attempt at treating me," Dex replied.

Becca smiled sheepishly. "I didn't know it would end up *that* big."

Zoey hid a smile. She had to give Becca a point for effort, though Dex's foot looked like a mummy.

"So what happened?" Max asked as he bent down to remove the bandage.

"Let me do it," Zoey said.

Zoey could see the look of shock on Dex's face. It seemed he had just noticed she was in the room. "Hello, ma'am," was all he said.

So this was how it was going to be. Pretending they'd never met? Why? The blind date wasn't supposed to be *that* big of a deal. Zoey straightened her shoulders. Well, two could play that game. Even though those two words from him had sent the butterflies in her stomach fluttering, Zoey pushed away the sensation.

She squatted and unwrapped the bandage until his ankle was exposed. It appeared slightly swollen, but it wasn't bruised. His feet didn't have that stinky smell she'd come to expect from guys. "So what happened here?" she asked in a brisk tone.

"I tripped while trying to move quickly," he said.

"He almost got stomped by the new horse and hurt his ankle while trying to get as far away from her as possible," Becca interjected.

Zoey's heart began to beat fast at the mention of the horse. She fought to keep her hands from shaking and forced herself to take a deep breath. Hopefully, no one would notice.

"So Lexi did this?" Max said.

"Max, why are you naming my horse?" Dex said. But all Zoey could think of was that incident many years ago—the one that had turned her life upside down. She forced herself to take another deep breath.

"You have a better name?"

"No."

"Then Lexi it is."

Becca chuckled. "These two... they never change. Always bickering like some old cackling hens." She glanced at Zoey. "Are you alright?" Becca asked so softly Zoey doubted the others heard, though Dex shot her a quick glance.

Zoey could feel her body finally calming down, and she quickly pasted a smile on her face. "I'm fine," she said.

"Did you just compare me to a fowl, darling?" Max said, his western drawl more prominent, distracting Becca, for which Zoey was grateful. She didn't need anyone digging deeper into her life.

"It was better than comparing you to a chicken," Becca replied.

Max made to grab her, but Becca laughed and slipped away. He tried again but to no avail.

"Hey, guys. Hello! I'm the patient, and I'm still here," Dex complained.

"You already have a doctor attending to you," Max said as he finally caught Becca and wrapped his arms around her before giving her a kiss on the cheek. "Quit whining."

Zoey hid a smile as Dex's ears grew warm. Apparently, he didn't appreciate the callout.

"On a scale of one to ten, how much does it hurt?" Zoey asked to distract him.

"A two? But I have a high tolerance for pain."

It sounded like a minor sprain, but it was best to make sure, given his pain tolerance level. "Anywhere else hurt?"

"No."

"Did you fall or hit your head?"

"No, just the tripping."

"I'm going to touch it now," she said. She palpated the skin around his ankle. There was some localized swelling, a little more than she'd expected for his level of pain, but Dex barely responded. "It doesn't hurt when I touch it?" she asked.

"Just a bit," he answered, his voice a little deeper.

"Are you alright?"

"You want to know the truth?"

She looked up at his face. "Sure."

He cleared his throat. "Your touch was soothing." Zoey noticed his neck turning red.

She couldn't help chuckling. Well, this was a first.

"What's funny?"

"Nothing. Do you think you could stand up and walk for me?"

"Yes, I can."

Zoey helped him bring down his foot from the coffee table, and Dex rose to his feet and took a few steps. He could bear weight on the injured ankle, though he limped a little. "How does the joint feel?" she asked.

"Relatively okay. Just some pain when I step on it."

"You can sit down now." She watched as he settled back on the couch.

"From what I can see, I doubt there's any fracture, and you probably only have an ankle sprain. But it's one you should take seriously. You need to make sure you don't cause any further damage, so no stomping around the ranch to take care of stuff."

Dex groaned. "That's going to be tough."

"I've already spoken to Fred, and he'll handle everything that needs to be taken care of," Max said. Zoey had no idea when he'd changed, but he now sported a jacket. "Fred is the ranch manager," he said for Zoey's benefit. "I also told him he had my permission to kick your butt, Dex, if he caught you doing anything."

"Thanks, Max," Zoey said. Turning back to Dex: "This isn't a joke. The ranch needs you to make sure your ankle heals well so you can get back to it. You need to rest this ankle for the next forty-eight hours, ice it for fifteen to twenty minutes three to five times a day, compress it with a bandage, and keep it elevated."

"Here's some ice," Becca said, handing over some already wrapped in a towel. Becca's hair was a little mussed-up, but Zoey said nothing and accepted the ice before pressing it against Dex's ankle. She heard him sigh with relief. "I brought some pain relievers too." Becca handed them to Dex with a small glass of water.

Dex swallowed both and returned the empty glass to her. "Thanks, Becca."

"Anytime."

Zoey turned to Max as she continued applying the ice. "I don't think he needs an X-ray or an MRI, but you might want to get one just to make sure everything is good with the ankle."

"I'll take care of it," Max said.

"I don't think he needs crutches, but a brace would be helpful."

"Here's one and another bandage." He handed both to Zoey. "Thank you so much for helping out, even though you didn't have to."

"It was my pleasure."

Max glanced at his watch. "Becca and I need to get going for me to make my meeting in Dexington, but I can't trust this big oaf to stay put long enough to ice his ankle."

"Hey—"

"It's true, Dex," Becca said. "It's hard for you to sit still."

"What if I help?" Zoey offered. "I can stay a little while to make sure he's all set." It wasn't a big deal, though she felt the butterflies in her stomach flutter at the thought of being alone with Dex.

"But what about Chloe?" Dex asked. "I promised Jax I'd tag-team watching her with him."

"Oh, please. Chloe can do without her favorite uncle for one day," Becca said.

"I also promised I'd play with her later," Zoey chimed in.

"Don't worry about it, Zoey. I'm sure there'll be more opportunities for that."

"It would be a good experience for Jax," Max said. "Time for him to try out being a daddy for a change. He's always busy or hurrying off somewhere."

"I've already sent him a quick text about it," Becca chimed in.

"Thanks," Dex said.

"Okay, we'll leave you guys to it." Max said. "Zoey, thanks again for coming. I'll get back to you soon."

"You're welcome."

"Zoey, it was great meeting you," Becca said.

"We should get together sometime if you don't mind."

Zoey liked Becca, and it would be nice to have one friend in this town. "I'll look forward to it."

"Why don't we exchange numbers?" Becca suggested. Zoey called out her digits and Becca saved them on her phone and then dialed Zoey's number to make sure she had hers. Zoey felt the vibration in her pants pocket. "Good. That's settled. I'll talk to you soon."

"Have a safe trip," Zoey said.

"Will do. C'mon, Max, let's go." She slipped her arm through his, and they headed to the door.

Zoey bent her head and began to study the packet the brace had come in.

"Oh, Zoey?"

Zoey turned in the direction of the door where Becca held the door open as Max waited outside for her. "Yes?"

"Could you stay for dinner? We'd love to have you."

CHAPTER 10

ex froze. Having Zoey here for an interview and helping him out was fine and dandy, but staying for dinner? What was Becca thinking? Dex was certain she was up to something.

"Okay, sure," Zoey said.

That quick? He couldn't imagine a beautiful woman like her spending the evening alone while on vacation. Surely she must already have plans for the evening. Didn't she mind being in such close quarters with his family after how the blind date had gone?

"Great," Becca said with a smile on her face. "I'll see you at seven." She closed the door behind her.

Dex let loose a breath. Thank goodness Becca and Max were gone. It had been hard keeping himself from glancing at Zoey every two seconds. Becca would have picked that up in a heartbeat.

But now they were alone in the house.

Together.

Dex felt his heart quicken at the thought. It wasn't the first time he'd been alone with a woman, so why did it suddenly feel warm when he was sure the air in the house was cool? He had to keep talking to distract his thoughts from going down a path they shouldn't.

"Thanks for helping me ice my foot," Dex said. "I think I can take it over from here."

"Are you sure?" Zoey asked.

"Positive."

"Show me."

Did she believe he couldn't do it? He accepted the towel-wrapped ice from her and leaned forward to reach his ankle. He grinned at Zoey, who had now taken the loveseat opposite him, as he pressed the ice against his leg. Easy peasy. That wasn't so hard, was it? Didn't Zoey know that cowboys were very flexible because of how much of a workout they got every day around the ranch?

A minute passed and then another minute.

The back of Dex's left calf began to tingle. He adjusted to ease his discomfort, but it didn't stop.

Then his lower back began to hurt, and finally, his hand started trembling.

Zoey burst out laughing. It was the sweetest sound he'd ever heard—rich, adorable, and carefree all rolled into one. Even though he could feel his ears warming up, Dex knew he would do anything to hear her laugh again.

"Hey, stop laughing at me," he said.

"Laughing at you? Why would I?" she said with feigned innocence, though a smile tugged at the corners of her lips.

"Alright, alright. I admit defeat," he said as he lowered his aching arm and leaned back.

Zoey laughed harder, her eyes twinkling with merriment.

Dex couldn't take his eyes off her. It was like he was mesmerized by this whole other unexpected side of her, one he wished he'd met first. Maybe the blind date had been just as awkward for her as it had been for him. Now he felt a strong draw to learn more about her. What made her tick?

"Tough cowboy, huh?" she said when her laughter finally died down.

"You won, alright?" he said, his shoulders relaxed.

She nodded. "I think we've iced your ankle

enough for now. Why don't I wrap it up for you and then help you get into the brace?"

"Sounds good," Dex said.

Zoey got up from her seat and then crouched near the coffee table. She wrapped the bandage around his ankle and slipped on the brace, then reached for a nearby throw-pillow and used it to elevate his ankle further.

"How does it feel?" she asked.

"Better. The pain meds must have kicked in too," Dex said.

"Great." She rose to her feet. "Could you point me in the direction of the bathroom? I need to wash my hands."

He gestured toward the mudroom. "We have a full bathroom through that door," he said.

"Thank you." She made her way there, her confident strides eating up the distance quickly. A few minutes later, she was back and had returned to the love seat.

"You have a beautiful home here," she said.

"Yes. I still love coming in here after all these years."

She glanced at him in surprise. "You don't live here?"

"I have my own property on the ranch. Max and his family live here in the main house."

"So why didn't you let them know we'd met before?"

Woah! That came out of left field. Had she felt hurt by it? He had to make sure she understood. "I figured you might not want the attention. Seeing you with Max made me realize you probably came for an interview. I didn't want their impression of you to be colored by whatever they might have heard about the blind date."

Zoey stiffened. "Did you tell them anything bad about me?"

"No, not me," he hurried to reassure her. "I'm sure you recall all the attention we had that day from all the other folks at the restaurant. Stories about us have probably made their way around town by now and might have reached Becca's ears. And you know how such stories can get twisted."

Her shoulders relaxed. "Okay, I get that."

"You may not have realized it, but this town is big on gossip. Especially with Miss Prissy.

Dex watched Zoey's face grow pale. "Miss Prissy?" she said. "Oh my."

"What's wrong? Oh, she probably set you up on the date."

"Not only that. I'm staying at her bed and breakfast. And I told her how the date went when she asked."

Ah! Now he understood how she'd been roped in even though she wasn't from this town. Miss Prissy could be very persistent when she wanted to be. But he had to know. "What did you tell her about the date?"

Zoey looked away. "That the date was a disaster."

Dex couldn't help laughing out loud.

Her eyes widened as they swung back to his. "You're not mad?"

"Why would I be? It's God's own truth about it."

"Sorry about the shirt."

He waved her concern away. "That was nothing. The shirt is fine now."

She let out a sigh. "That date was so awkward. Then there were those interruptions. You didn't help with all the monosyllabic answers you gave. It felt like you wanted to be anywhere else but with me."

He adjusted in his seat. "Oh, it was definitely awkward," he said. "I wished the date had been more private. I didn't speak much because I was starstruck with how beautiful you were."

Zoey blushed and seemed lost for words. "How

can you say things like that with a straight face?" she finally said.

He grinned. "It's true. I thought so at the restaurant and also on the first day we met."

Zoey covered her face with her hands. "Oh, please don't remind me about the grocery store. That was so embarrassing!"

"I was just glad I said something before most folks noticed."

She dropped her hands. "I thought everyone was looking at me."

"I think they were more interested in seeing us together than in what had actually happened."

"Why? Are you a celebrity of some sort in this town?"

"Not quite. But you might have noticed that my brother and I share the same last name as this town. My family were the first settlers in this area, so the town got named after them. That tends to bring some extra attention wherever we're concerned."

"You sound like you don't care for it."

Dex steepled his fingers together. "I'm a very private man, even more so than my brothers." He glanced at her. "Does that bother you?"

"Why should it? We all have our likes and dislikes."

"What about you? What do you dislike?"

Zoey burrowed further into the cushy leather love seat. Then her face turned serious. "I'd like no betrayals. I like people to be upfront with me so I can trust that what I'm seeing is who they really are."

There had to be a story there. For some reason, his pulse raced at the thought that someone might have hurt her before. But this was not the time to question her about it.

He spread out his arms over the top of the couch and gave her a warm smile. "It's nice talking to you like this."

Her face brightened. "I know. Who would have thought? You're pretty verbal for someone I had just about written off as a recluse."

Dex chuckled. "Recluse? Me? I'm private, but not *that* private."

She grinned. "Good to know."

"Forgive my manners. Would you like anything to drink?" he asked.

"I'd like some water."

"Let me—"

"Stop. Don't move. It's in the kitchen, right?" The living, dining, and kitchen areas shared an open floor layout, so Zoey could see the kitchen from where she sat.

"Yes, it's in the refrigerator. We also have filtered tap water if you'd prefer that."

"I'll get it."

Zoey rose and made her way to the kitchen. She soon returned with two glasses of water and handed one to him. "Here you go."

"Thank you," he said. Dex waited until she was seated and then downed his. The cool, refreshing water soothed his dry throat. He hadn't realized how much he needed a drink.

He dropped the glass on the coffee table. "I hope I'm not taking too much of your time," he said.

She shook her head. "I'm on vacation. This was sort of an impromptu trip, so I don't have much planned."

That explained why she'd been quick to take up Becca's dinner offer. But did her coming here for an interview mean there was a possibility she would stay in Dexin Valley? For some reason, the thought of that thrilled him.

"So, do you enjoy working on a ranch?" she asked.

"I do. I love everything about it. The horses, the cattle, the people, the land. It's hard work and fun at the same time. Have you ever been on a ranch before?"

"I have, when I was little."

His heart jumped with hope when she said that. It meant she'd probably seen the reality of a ranch before and not just what most people thought it was like. He wanted to know more, but from the change in the tone of her voice, it seemed it was something she didn't really want to speak further on. Dex decided to change the subject. "So, about dinner tonight."

"Oh no! Did I put you in a tough spot by accepting?"

Dex shook his head. "Not at all. It seems Becca likes you."

"I like her too. And Chloe."

"You met her? She's a hoot."

"And cute as a button."

"She's definitely more than just cute. Wait until you become a target of her antics."

"But you love her."

"You can't help it. She brings in so much sunshine."

"I'm guessing she'll be there at dinner."

"Yes, as well as my other brother, Jax."

She peered at him curiously. "So how many brothers do you have?"

"Three. Max, Jax, and Rex."

"Won't Rex be at the dinner too?"

"He lives in another state."

"Oh."

Dex prayed she wouldn't ask more about him. Talking about Rex was a touchy subject in their house. "And just so you know, it might be best if you don't mention Rex's name at the dinner," he said.

"Okay." He was glad she didn't probe more.

"So what should I wear for the dinner?" she asked.

"Mealtimes are very casual here, so you can wear whatever you feel comfortable in."

"Okay." She lifted her glass and took a sip.

They stayed silent for a moment, but it wasn't awkward. A part of him wished they could have more moments like this. He was liking her more and more.

Zoey finished her drink and picked up both glasses.

"You don't have to do that," Dex said.

She shrugged. "It's not a big deal. I'll be right back."

Zoey headed to the kitchen. A few moments later, he could hear her rinsing off the glasses. Soon she returned. "I have to go now," she said. "I'd like to see more of the town today."

"I wish I could help. It's always nice to have a handy travel guide."

She chuckled. "Thanks for the offer, but taking care of your ankle is your number one priority now." She picked up her satchel that had been resting on the arm of the loveseat. "It was great chatting with you, Dex."

"Same here." He lifted his leg from the coffee table and placed it on the floor.

"Oh no, you don't have to see me off."

"I have to, or my Ma will come from the grave and have my hide. Besides, I need to move about sooner or later."

"Okay, but you have to agree to let me help you."

Now, that was an offer he had no plans to refuse. Dex got to his feet as Zoey slung the satchel over her left shoulder and moved to stand beside him. Her soft, subtle scent washed over him, and he fought the urge to breathe it in.

"Now put your arm over my shoulder," she said.

Dex obeyed and then leaned toward her. His frame seemed to dwarf hers, but she didn't even stumble—she was much stronger than she appeared. There was a certain electricity in the air from her nearness, and his skin tingled where it touched hers. It took everything in him not to touch her hair that grazed his arm. He could only imagine how soft it was.

He took one step then another with her support. Truth be told, he could probably have made his way alone to the door, but he was enjoying her closeness too much to insist otherwise.

They reached the door and then stepped out. "I'll stop right here," he said.

"Okay." She waited for him to lift his arm, then she stepped away.

"Can I have your number?" Dex hoped she wouldn't rebuff him.

"It's about time," she said with a smile.

"What do you mean?"

"You didn't ask for it when I wanted to leave at the end of the date."

"I wasn't sure how you'd feel about that," Dex said. "It was as if you'd written the date off when you insisted you had to leave, so I didn't want to complicate matters for you."

She looked him straight in the eye. "Dex, a lady always wants you to ask for her number. Then it becomes her choice to turn you down or not."

"So, pretty lady, can I have your number?"

Zoey laughed. "Yes, you can. You're so full of surprises. I'm glad I met this Dex today."

"Me too." Zoey laughed again. Dex's ears warmed. "I mean, I'm glad I met you," he finished.

"Let me have your phone," she said.

Dex pulled out his phone from his jean pocket, unlocked it, and handed it to her. She punched in a couple of digits, and then he heard her phone buzz in her satchel.

"We're all set," she said.

"Thank you."

"I have it saved as 'the pretty lady' on your phone."

Dex chuckled. "Now I wonder what you'll save mine as."

"That's a secret." She winked at him.

Dex's lips turned up in a smile. "Thanks for spending time with me."

"You're welcome. See you later." She waved at him and then strode to her car at the end of the parking space.

Dex watched as she drove off. Zoey had turned out more interesting than he'd first thought.

He couldn't wait to see how dinner with her would go.

CHAPTER 11

"Thank you so much for coming," Becca said as she hugged Zoey. "You look fantastic."

Zoey's face warmed. She'd followed Dex's advice and was now dressed in a cotton floral-print blouse with long bishop sleeves tucked in the front into skinny jeans. Her hair was done up in a loose top-knot bun, and she'd even managed to dab a bit of lip gloss on her lips. "Thank you. I'm happy to be here," she responded. "Here's something for you." She handed over the chocolate cake she'd bribed Miss Prissy to bake.

"This looks wonderful! The guys will be so happy about this," she said as she accepted the cake. "Come on in. Everyone is already here."

"I thought dinner was supposed to be at seven?" Zoey had arrived a few minutes early just in case.

Becca laughed. "The crew seems to be super hungry today, but we haven't started yet," she said as she led the way to the dining area. "Let me introduce you to everyone."

Max was seated at the head of the large farmhouse dining table, with Chloe on his immediate right. Dex and another young man, who Zoey presumed to be Jax, were on his left. Chloe had on a pretty yellow dress, while the guys were dressed nicely in jeans and button-down shirts. But Zoey only had eyes for Dex. It had to be illegal for him to look that good.

"Hello, Zoey," Dex said in that voice that turned her insides to mush. He got up and walked over to Chloe's side with a less noticeable limp than before, pulling out the seat next to where Zoey presumed was Becca's place.

Max and the other young man got to their feet. "Welcome," Max said. "Glad you could join us."

"Thanks for inviting me," Zoey said.

"And I'm Jax, younger brother to these two," the young man said with a large smile on his face as he gestured to Max and Dex. "And yes, our Ma had a love for the letter X."

"Nice to meet you, Jax," Zoey said. She'd wondered about the 'X' connection.

"Hi," Chloe said with a shy smile.

"Hello, Chloe." Zoey gave her a small wave.

"And Zoey brought chocolate cake," Becca said.

"Nice," Jax said. "How did she know it's a favorite in this house?"

"Why don't we all take our seats?" Max said.

"I'll drop the cake in the kitchen and be right back," Becca said. "Don't wait for me." But Zoey had a feeling these guys would, no matter what Becca had said.

Zoey headed to where Dex was waiting and sat down with his assistance. "Thank you," she said. "How is your ankle doing?"

"Much better, as long as I don't try to run." Then he made his way back to his seat and sat down. For some reason, sitting opposite him was making butterflies pop up in her stomach, yet she couldn't imagine having it any other way.

The table was already piled high with food, and the smell caused Zoey's stomach to rumble.

Her ears warmed. She hoped no one else had heard the noise. A quick look around the table showed no one had. Well, except for Dex, who had a smile playing at the corners of his lips.

Zoey could feel the warmth creeping up her face. Why did he have to witness every embarrassing moment of hers? He must have seen the emotion on her face because he suddenly said: "Jax, did you make sure that Lexi's stall was all locked up?"

"That goes without saying," Jax replied. "I triple-checked just in case."

"Thanks."

"I'm hungry," Chloe said.

"Give Mommy a minute, okay?" Max said.

"Okay." She started playing with a cloth doll she'd kept by her side.

Somehow, Zoey couldn't take her eyes away from the food. She hadn't realized she was that hungry. And she loved hot food—she could see the steam still rising from some of the dishes.

"We brought out the food as soon as Becca went to the door for you," Dex said quietly.

"More like I brought out the dishes while you warmed your tush in the seat," Jax interjected.

Zoey hid a smile. Jax was definitely the more outspoken one. It seemed he had no issues saying what was on his mind.

"I'm the patient," Dex said to Jax. "Doctor's orders." He winked at Zoey.

"Oh, please," Jax said. "This is why we don't let

Dex fall sick, Zoey. He'll probably milk it for all it's worth."

Dex shrugged. "Not my fault."

Becca returned at that moment, and the quibbling came to an end. Max led them in a brief prayer before they dove in.

The food was amazing. There was beef stew with root vegetables that warmed the soul, baked potatoes topped with sour cream, gooey cheddar cheese, bits of mushroom, and shredded carrots that Zoey couldn't stop eating, spicy slow-cooked ribs that were so finger-licking good the meat practically fell off the bone by itself, and a yummy cheesy bean casserole. Dessert was topped off with the chocolate cake Zoey had brought that was so delicious she wasn't surprised at the speed with which Dex and Jax tucked it in. She was pretty sure their metabolism would burn it all away with the amount of ranch work they did.

"Ah, this was so good," Jax said. "Zoey, thanks for the cake." He leaned back with a satisfied smile on his face.

"You're welcome," she replied. "It was courtesy of Miss Prissy."

"That woman is a cooking fiend," Jax said.

"Yes, she is," Becca agreed.

Zoey turned to her. "Thanks for the wonderful dinner. It was delicious." By now, everyone had finished eating.

"Oh, it wasn't me. It was all Dex," Becca said.

"Mommy! What about me?" Chloe chimed in.

"Well, with Chloe's assistance," Becca corrected.

"Good job, Chloe," Zoey said with a smile. Chloe beamed proudly. Then Zoey turned to Dex. "Thanks for the meal. But weren't you supposed to be laying off your feet?"

"I did," Dex replied with feigned innocence on his face. "I prepped most of it sitting down."

Jax grunted. "More like he was giving out the commands, and we were the foot soldiers doing all the work," he said.

"No, he was the prince, and Uncle Jax was the butler, like in the story you read to me, Mommy," Chloe stated loudly. "And I was the princess, right, Uncle Dex?"

"Yes, you sure were, Chloe."

"See? This is why I can't win against these two." Jax pretended to pout. "Always banding together."

Chloe giggled and stuck out her tongue. "That's for eating my cookie, Uncle Jax."

"Hey! It was only a tiny bit! And you had five others."

"It was mine," Chloe said as she crossed her arms over her chest. "You didn't say please."

"You didn't ask before eating it, Jax?" Becca said.

"I did," Jax said in his defense. "She just didn't hear me."

"Same thing," Max said.

"Sorry, Chloe," Jax said.

"Okay. I forgive you," she said in a chirpy voice.

"Thank you, Your Majesty." Jax executed a bow.

Chloe giggled again and then yawned.

"I see it's someone's bedtime," Becca said to Chloe.

"Please, Mommy, I want to stay with Aunt Zuzu. If I go to bed, Aunt Zuzu will go away."

Zoey chuckled. Now, that was a new one. She'd been given different nicknames over the years but never Zuzu. She liked it. "You could always tell your mom anytime you want to see me, Chloe," she said.

"Really?" She was practically bouncing. "Now I'm ready for story time!"

"Everyone hold on," Becca stated.

All eyes turned to her.

Her face turned serious. "I have some very important news," she said.

CHAPTER 12

*D*ex had enjoyed having Zoey at dinner. He'd kept peeking at her as if to reassure himself that she was actually here. And she looked stunning. Somehow he'd wished the dinner would never end. But all that was now forgotten at he stared at Becca.

His heart began to pound. Was this about the doctor's appointment she'd had earlier today? She'd said nothing when Leah's driver had dropped her off, so he'd assumed everything was alright.

Dex hoped it wasn't terrible news. He couldn't imagine anything happening to Becca. Even though she hadn't been in their lives for long, she was like the glue that held them together with her sunny personality and generous heart. The only times he'd felt the way he did right now were when Max had gotten into an accident and when Ma had broken the news of her sickness to him and his brothers. *God, please, let this not be the same*, he prayed.

"What is it, sweetheart?" Max asked, his attention focused solely on Becca. Dex couldn't imagine how he must be feeling right now, though he managed to maintain a calm demeanor.

"Well, I've been forgetting stuff recently and have been getting so tired lately that I decided to see a doctor earlier today," Becca said.

"That's why you went with me to Dexington?" Max said.

"Yes, in addition to the upcoming triple wedding stuff I'd said I was working on. I'm sorry I didn't tell you. I didn't want you to worry."

Max reached out for her hand and placed it in his. "It's always better for us to worry together. So what did the doctor say?"

"That you have to get an extra bed."

"What?" everyone except Chloe chorused.

"Max, we're having a baby." Her eyes brimmed with tears.

Max froze like a deer in headlights. Jax's mouth hung open so wide Dex worried a fly would get in. Zoey was beaming. Well, Chloe was just Chloe. She probably didn't understand what her mom had just said. Dex, on the other hand, let out a sigh of relief. It was better news than he'd expected.

Then Max jumped to his feet, strode to where Becca sat, and then lifted her into his arms.

"Max, put me down!" she protested.

Max then sealed her lips with a kiss that went on for so long Dex had to look away. Zoey, on the other hand, blushed to the roots of her hair.

"Daddy!" Chloe called out.

Max came back to his senses. "Oh, sorry," he said with a sheepish grin.

"No need to apologize," Jax said. "We're used to it. It's not like you won't do it again." Dex wished he could plug Jax's mouth, or anything to get him to stop talking. Couldn't he see they had a guest here? But Jax carried on as if he didn't have a care in the world. "Becca, congratulations! You almost gave us a heart attack. You can't do stuff like that to us."

"I'm sorry," Becca said with a smile. She gestured at Max to put her down, which he did.

"Congrats, Becca," Zoey said.

"Thank you, Zoey," she replied. "I hope I didn't embarrass you with my news."

Zoey shook her head. "It's the best news ever."

Dex rose to his feet and strode over to where

Becca stood. He wrapped his arms around her. "I'm so glad you're okay," he said. "Congratulations!" Then he whispered: "Max is freaking out."

"I'm not," Max insisted vehemently. "This is the best news ever. Now, let go of my wife."

Dex released her and placed a hand on Max's shoulder. "Max, it's okay to freak out. We all realize this is your first rodeo at this thing, despite Chloe."

"Yeah, Max. It's okay if you do," Jax concurred.

"You guys are nuts." Max turned to Becca. "Thank you so much for this wonderful gift. Are you okay? Is there anything I can do? Maybe it's better if you sit down."

Jax glanced at Dex, and they both nodded in agreement. "Totally freaking out."

"Mommy, am I getting a little baby?" Chloe said.

Everyone chuckled. Chloe definitely had a way with words.

Becca turned to her and crouched by her side. "You're going to have a baby sister or brother."

"Really?"

"Really."

"Thank you, Mommy. Will she fart?" Chloe wrinkled her nose in disgust at the thought.

Jax snickered, while Zoey hid a smile. Dex wondered if Chloe would sleep through tonight with all the ideas and thoughts he was pretty sure were already bouncing around in her head.

"I think we'll leave that discussion for another day," Max said. "Come on, Chloe. It's time for bed."

"But I'm not tired," she protested. Then she yawned again.

Becca stepped away so Max could lift Chloe into his arms. "Come on, sweetheart, let's go." He turned to Zoey. "It was great having you here tonight. Feel free to stop by anytime you like. You're always welcome."

"Thanks for having me," Zoey responded. "Goodnight, Chloe."

"Goodnight, Mommy, Aunt Zuzu." She let out another yawn. "Goodnight, Uncle Jax, Uncle Dex."

Max carried her off in the direction of their wing.

Becca turned to Zoey. "Would you like some coffee?"

Zoey smiled. "Coffee sounds good."

"I'll get it," Jax said. "Becca, you have to take things easy from now. Just let Dex and me know if you need anything."

Becca waved away his concern. "I'll be fine."

"We won't be," Jax replied. "And Maggie will have our hides if she finds out we let you lift anything more than a finger. Consider us your workhorses from now on." He moved away to the kitchen.

Maggie would certainly give them a hard time. It didn't matter how old they were now—they were still kids as far as she was concerned. "Have you told Maggie?" Dex asked.

"No, I wanted to tell Max and you guys first. I also feel like she would cut short her honeymoon if she heard I was pregnant. She deserves the time away. I'd prefer to keep the news until she gets back."

Dex shook his head. "That won't work. Chloe will tell her the first chance she gets. Make Maggie promise first that she won't come running back, and then tell her the news. You know she'll keep her word no matter what."

"Okay, I'll do that. I'll also let my sister and her family know tomorrow."

"I thought she went with you to the appointment."

"No, she didn't. I wanted Max to be the first to know."

"How are you feeling?" Zoey asked.

"A little tired but happy. It feels surreal. You'd think I would have known I was pregnant, considering I've gone through this before."

"How far along are you?"

"I'll find out for sure tomorrow when I go back with Max for the first scan. But they think I might be as far along as eight weeks."

"I wish you all the best with the pregnancy."

"Thank you. I went through it alone with Chloe, so it's nice that I get to go through it with family by my side."

"It sure is," Max said. He'd returned back to the living room.

"Is Chloe already asleep?" Becca asked.

"Didn't even make it through her prayers. Fell asleep as soon as her head hit the pillow."

By now, Jax had returned with a tray filled with mugs of steaming black coffee. He placed it in the center of the table. "Please help yourself. There's sugar and milk, Zoey, if you need those."

"Thank you," Zoey said.

"You're always welcome," Jax said, giving Zoey the warmest smile Dex had ever seen on his face.

Dex felt a pang of jealousy as he watched their exchange. Was Jax flirting with Zoey? For some reason, he didn't want his younger brother anywhere near her or giving her that extra special smile.

He sighed with relief when Jax's attention turned to Becca as he lifted a glass of milk and passed it to her. "This one is for you," Jax said. "I hereby declare you on a coffee ban until the baby comes."

Becca groaned. "I'm sure I can still have one cup of coffee."

"I'm with Jax on this one, sweetheart," Max said, rubbing her back. "You can do this."

"Hmmm. That feels good," Becca said, closing her eyes briefly in pleasure. "But I ain't giving up yet on that coffee."

Zoey burst out laughing, the sound sweeter to Dex's ears than before. He had a feeling he would never get tired of it. He watched as she finished her cup of coffee and then rose to her feet.

"I have to go," she said. "Thank you so much for the wonderful dinner and company."

"We enjoyed having you here," Jax said.

Dex got to his feet. "I'll see you to the door," he said.

"I'll come with you," Becca said. "Max, you stay. I'll be right back."

Dex led the way to the door while Becca chatted with Zoey behind him. Soon they were out in the cool night air.

"So, Dex," Becca began just as Zoey turned towards her car, "when were you planning on telling me that Zoey was your blind date?"

CHAPTER 13

Zoey was at a loss for words. She'd been relieved when no one had mentioned the blind date at dinner—she'd wrongly assumed they'd known nothing about it.

Dex froze but soon quickly regained his composure. "I didn't think it was a big deal," he said as he leaned against the wall, his hands in his jeans' pockets.

"How did you find out?" Zoey asked.

"Miss Prissy called and told me all about it," Becca said.

"That woman and her big mouth," Dex murmured.

Zoey hid her smile. Those were Zoey's same thoughts, though in more appropriate words. Miss

Prissy was a sweet woman, but her mouth ran faster than an express train. It seemed her reputation was well-earned.

"What did you say?" Becca asked.

"Nothing," Dex replied.

"So is it bygones now between you two?" Becca asked, looking from Zoey to Dex and then back to Zoey.

Dex glanced at Zoey with a look that communicated he expected her to respond. She liked that he'd left it up to her to define what was going on between them. "I think we've decided to be friends for now," Zoey said, watching for Dex's reaction.

He nodded in agreement. "Definitely friends."

"Good," Becca said with a sigh of relief. "Because I'd really like you to be my friend, Zoey, and it would have been hard to do so if things were ugly between you two." She straightened. "I do have a favor."

"What is it?" Zoey asked.

"Are you free tomorrow morning?"

Right now, she had nothing on her schedule. It was truly a wake-up-in-the-morning-and-decide type of vacation. "Yes. Why do you ask?"

"Would you like to join me tomorrow and meet the girls?"

"Girls?"

"I probably haven't mentioned it, but I'm a part-time wedding planner," Becca said. "I'm planning a triple wedding for my niece and her two friends. They're all residents at Dexington Medical. Would you like to join us?"

That sounded fun. Zoey had never even heard of a triple wedding, let alone been part of the planning of one. "Are you sure?"

"Don't worry. I'm sure you'll fit right in. The more the merrier, and you ladies can talk shop if you want."

"What time?"

"Nine a.m. The ladies like to start early."

"Okay, I'll come."

"Thank you!"

"Ugh. That means I have to make myself scarce around the house tomorrow," Dex said.

Zoey glanced at him. "Why?"

Becca chuckled. "Five ladies in one place is too much for these guys. You should see how Max disappears when they come. And that's not even the full gang. We haven't counted in the mothers, mothers-in-law, and grandma."

Dex stiffened. "Grandma Helen isn't coming, is she?"

Becca laughed out loud. "No, she isn't. Aw, don't worry, your poor cheeks are safe." Then to Zoey: "Grandma Helen is one of the most wonderful women I've ever met. She's the biological grandmother to one of the girls' fiancés and the resident grandma to everyone else. She just has a thing for Dex's cheeks."

The imagery of a lady pinching Dex's cheeks was too hilarious, and Zoey chuckled.

"Hey, it's not funny," Dex protested.

"Sorry," Zoey said. But the mental picture of Dex running away from the cheek-pinching lady chasing closely behind was too much, and Zoey burst out laughing. Becca joined in. "I'm so sorry, I'm really sorry," Zoey said once the laughter had died down. "Those poor cheeks of yours must really hurt whenever it happens."

Dex straightened from where he'd been leaning, a playful glint in his eyes. "Maybe I could demonstrate for you, using your cheeks as an example."

Zoey took a few steps back as she covered her cheeks in mock horror. "No thank you."

"Are you sure?" Dex took a step toward her. "Experience can be the best teacher."

Zoey took another step backward. "Consider the lesson learned."

"I thought so."

"Alright, alright. Calm down, everyone," Becca said. "Tomorrow will be a fun time, Zoey. I promise."

"I'll be here," Zoey said.

"I look forward to it. I have to go in now. Have a wonderful night and thank you again for coming." She turned into the house and shut the door behind her.

Dex gave Zoey a small smile. "I hope my family wasn't too much tonight."

Zoey shook her head. "I had fun, and the food was delicious. It's been a while since I had this type of dinner."

Dex looked at her curiously. "You don't go home often?"

"I do sometimes." But that was all Zoey planned to say about it—she didn't want to talk about her family, at least not tonight. She gestured to her car. "I have to go now."

"I'll walk you over." Dex strolled beside her in companionable silence, slowing his stride until it was in rhythm with hers. Then she reached the driver's side of her car. She unlocked the door, which he then opened for her.

"Thank you," Zoey said.

"Do you like horses?" he asked out of the blue.

Zoey's breath hitched. "Yes ..." That was the truth. But where was Dex going with this? Her heart began to beat faster.

"Would you like to check out the horses with me tomorrow once you're done with the ladies?"

Zoey's breath quickened as memories of the past came flooding back.

She forced herself to stay calm. She couldn't keep running from the past forever. Maybe this was a good time to face her memories. And truth be told, a part of her leaped at the chance to touch those majestic beasts again. It wasn't really about the fact that she would have more alone time with Dex and get a chance to know more about this man that was affecting her in ways she'd never expected. "I'd like that."

His face creased into a smile. "Great."

She slid into the car. He closed the door after her and stepped away.

Zoey started the ignition, gave him a small wave, and drove off.

But she wasn't sure if her visit tomorrow would be liberating, or if it would end up in yet another disaster.

CHAPTER 14

"You must be in a great mood if you're whistling," a voice said.

Dex jumped back and then adjusted his stance to steady himself. "Becca! I could have hurt my ankle just now!"

She stepped out into the light where he could see her.

Becca chuckled. "Sorry. I couldn't help myself."

"What's going on?"

"I wanted to chat with you for a bit."

Dex leaned against the wall. "What about?"

"You and Zoey. You like her, don't you?"

Becca was as perceptive as ever. There was no need to hide how he felt. "I do."

"Are you going to pursue her?"

He glanced at her. "I'd like to. No, I'm going to."

Becca nodded. "Good. Something tells me she's special." Becca rubbed the back of her ear. "But I think she might have been hurt before." She wriggled a finger at Dex. "So don't play games with her or hurt her."

"You know I won't do that. But how did you know? Did she tell you anything?"

Becca shook her head. "I can see it in her eyes. When you've gone through some stuff before, it's very easy to see the signs."

"I plan to take things slow."

"That's fine, but don't move so slowly that you lose her. Sometimes you have to take a leap of faith. She's a good one, and I bet lots of folks are interested in her."

Dex looked at her sharply. "Did you hear anything from Miss Prissy?"

"Isn't Zoey gorgeous enough that everyone would want her?"

Oh, she was definitely stunning. "That she is. But it's important for me to really get to know and understand her. I also need to be sure she'll accept me for who I am: a cowboy at heart."

Becca patted his arm. "Any woman would be lucky to have you. Don't worry, I doubt she's one of those superficial ladies. She'll let you know if she's interested or not." She stifled a yawn. "Time for me to call it a night."

"Thanks for the chat, Becca."

"You're welcome. That's what big sisters do."

Dex chuckled. Big sister? Yes, she definitely acted like one. But maybe even more bossy. "Is Jax done with the dishes?"

"Yes, he and Max took care of it. So you don't have to come back in if you don't want to."

"I think I'll take you up on that offer and head home."

"More like you want to avoid Jax's twenty questions."

Dex chuckled. Becca could read him too well. "That too. Goodnight, Becca."

"Goodnight." Dex watched as she entered the house.

Then he turned and began the walk back to his place.

It had been a wonderful evening. Spending time with his family was always great, but Zoey being there had been like the icing on the cake. She'd seemed to fit in well with them, which he liked. The last thing he needed was to date a woman who didn't care for his family. Sure, they were a quirky lot, just like he was, but they were kind and were always there for each other when it mattered.

But he was most excited by the chance to spend more time with her tomorrow.

Dex couldn't wait to see what the next day would bring.

CHAPTER 15

Zoey pressed the bell. A moment later, the door swung open, and Becca stood there wearing a big smile. "Hello, Zoey." Becca waved her in.

"I hope I'm not late," Zoey said as she stepped into the house.

"Not at all."

A car horn blasted from behind them.

Zoey turned to see a black limousine come to a stop in front of the house.

The door opened, and three ladies stepped out, each one beautiful in her own way. The one with the lovely dark hair could pass for a model with her tall, lithe figure, the second was petite with sun-kissed blonde hair cut into a pixie style, while the third was about Zoey's height and had gorgeous red hair pulled into a loose ponytail.

"Hello, Aunt Becca," the third one called out with a big smile on her face as she hurried over and gave Becca a hug. She had to be Becca's niece. The resemblance between them was definitely there, but the flashing green eyes sealed the deal. "Oh, you have a visitor."

"Hello, girls," Becca said as she gave each one a hug. "Meet Zoey, my new friend. Zoey, meet Jasmine, my niece, Alicia, and Dana."

New friend. Zoey liked the sound of that.

"Hello!" the trio replied.

"Hi," Zoey said. "It's nice to meet you all."

"I invited her to spend the time with us," Becca said. "Hope you don't mind."

"Any friend of Becca's is a friend of ours," Alicia said with a smile.

"True," Dana concurred.

"Okay, let's go inside and we can talk more." Becca led the way through the living room to her home office.

"This is nice," Zoey said as she looked around. The place had a sense of understated luxury with its light blue and gold accents, yet it was cheery at the same time. And the air held faint notes of a calming flowery scent. Zoey liked what Becca had done with the space. The group settled on the couch and seats in the client consultation area.

"Thank you," Becca responded. "It's my own tiny world on this ranch."

"Tiny?" Jasmine said with a raised eyebrow. "Zoey, you need to see her wardrobe. I'm sure Max is drowning in all the shoes she has in there."

"Not to mention the bags," Dana chimed in.

"And the clothes," Jasmine and Alicia said together.

"And that's just in this home. It's even worse at their Dexington house," Jasmine finished.

"Hey! There's nothing wrong with having enough clothes," Becca said with a smile. "I'm not like you folks who practically live in the hospital for half your lives. I've got places to go."

"Thanks for the dig, Aunt Becca," Jasmine said.

"I hate when she calls me that," Becca said to Zoey. "Makes me feel old."

Zoey smiled in return. This trio was definitely a riot, but they seemed close and comfortable with each other. Zoey wished she had a friendship group like this in her life.

"What about Chloe?" Alicia asked.

"Max took her out for a visit to see her friends on

a playdate at a nearby ranch. They'll be back in a few hours."

"Aw, that's so sweet of him," Dana said.

"I miss her," Becca said. "But it's nice to have some girl time."

"It sure is," Alicia said.

"So, Zoey, what did you specialize in?" Dana asked.

"Emergency Medicine Ultrasound fellowship."

"Nice," Jasmine said. "Ultrasounds are the bane of my existence. Any chance you could join the family?"

"What do you mean?" Zoey asked.

"Jasmine, you need to ask the right question," Dana scolded. "So are you single, Zoey?"

"Oh, leave her alone," Becca said. "It's not like you have brothers or anything. Last time I checked, you were an only child."

"True," Jasmine agreed. "I don't have brothers." She leaned forward. "But I know who does," she said in a conspiratorial tone.

Alicia glanced at Jasmine. "Who?"

"Cut!" Becca said. "I'm going to end this conversation right here. Jasmine, you're not allowed to badger my friend."

"Me? I'm as innocent as a kitten," Jasmine

responded. Then she leaned back. "Now why do I feel like you're hiding something, Aunt Becca?"

"What do you mean?"

"Hmmm. I can smell something fishy, like someone is cooking something up."

Becca shook her head. "What's wrong with her today?" she asked Alicia.

Alicia laughed. "I don't know. Maybe she hasn't come down from the high of kissing a *certain* somebody multiple times yesterday."

Jasmine blushed. "Hey! Don't go there. This could turn into a bloodbath if we head down that road. All your secrets could spontaneously erupt. Besides, it's not my fault. I can't help that he's a great kisser."

Zoey just watched their exchange with amusement. It was like watching a live soap opera with no end in sight.

"Okay, settle down," Becca said. "Let's talk about the weddings."

"We're getting married on the same day in three different weddings," Dana said to Zoey.

A logistical nightmare the more she thought about it!

"I know what you're thinking," Dana continued. "But if anyone can pull it off, it's Becca. She's a well-known event planner for celebrities. A former socialite."

Becca brushed her praise aside. "I don't do much of that anymore. I just prefer to plan weddings and deal with bridezillas like these three."

"Hey!" they chorused.

Becca chuckled. Then her face turned serious. She flipped open a file she'd pulled out earlier. "So, we're all set with the wedding dresses and maids of honor dresses."

"I think I might have lost weight," Dana said. "I've worked long hours these past few weeks in the OR."

"Okay, we'll do a final check for measurements two weeks before the wedding, and we can make any adjustments. In the meantime, try not to lose any more weight. You ladies are skinny enough as it is. I'd like healthy-looking brides please."

"We could have the dress rehearsal as another slumber party," Dana suggested. "The last one we had with Alicia's wedding dress was so much fun."

"Sure, as long as I'm not the one planning it," Becca said.

"The timing might be tight right now," Alicia said. "How about we have a regular slumber party after we get back from our honeymoons?" she suggested. "We can have all the ladies over."

A ladies' slumber party? That sounded like so much fun.

"Ooh, I like that," Jasmine said. "That's better than a slumber party before the wedding, which I really think would drive Aunt Becca bonkers."

They all burst out laughing. Zoey couldn't remember when she'd last had so much fun like this with other ladies. She had her friend, Tara, but no one else as close.

"Okay, moving on." Becca scanned the paper in front of her. "Have you made a decision on who the groomsmen and bridesmaids would be?"

Alicia glanced at Dana and Jasmine before answering. "We decided we won't have any. We'll be each other's maids of honor—we'll change between ceremonies, and that should be enough. Instead, we've elected to go with the same dress code idea for our friends. We've seen the fabric Aunt Leah's couture partner came up with, and we love it. And it's all organic too. I sent you a list of our friends who'll be getting outfits from it on our way here. It should be in your inbox now."

"Okay, I'll check it later," Becca said. "We should have them going in for measurements and to select their design preference starting next week, so the outfits can be made on time."

"That should work," Jasmine said. "We've already given them a heads-up, and they're excited about it."

"And the guys are covering the costs," Dana said.

"Awesome," Becca said. "Next on the list, RSVPs. They've all been sent out, and we've already gotten back sixty percent of responses. I expect that to go up in the next week or two."

"Yes, Blake's mom told me she'd heard back from all the most important folks like close friends and family," Alicia said. "We are more or less waiting to hear from those on the other side of the country."

"Blake is Alicia's fiancé," Dana whispered to Zoey.

"So how is the RSVP working with three weddings?" Zoey asked.

"We agreed to have Sarah, Alicia's mother-in-law-to-be, manage all the RSVPs," Jasmine said. "Dana's and Alicia's parents have passed away, and my parents have a lot on their plate right now with the expansion of their lingerie business. But all the moms and mom representatives from both sides meet once a week to discuss the wedding."

"That sounds organized," Zoey said.

"It is," Becca said. "And it gives me one less thing to worry about." She looked at her list. "The wedding and reception are at the Dexington estate. I'm working with Grandma Helen on that. Of course, there will be tight security. I have a team already in place. Each of you, as well as your grooms, will get a changing room. Jasmine's mom is handling pre-wedding pictures, some of which are for the press release and magazines."

"Ugh. That's the part I don't like," Dana said. "I enjoy my current anonymity."

"Sorry. It's all Alicia's fault," Becca said. "She had to fall in love with the city's darling royalty. It's the only way to make sure the paparazzi don't infringe on the ceremony itself. That's the legal agreement we have in place with them." She glanced at her list again. "The photographer, videographer, caterer, florist, and musicians are all taken care of. We have back-ups ready for those as well."

Becca continued to go down the list, taking care of one item after the other and making notes. How was she able to keep all these straight? Zoey was exhausted just listening to it all.

"Why don't we take a break?" Becca said after some time. "I'll be right back."

"Do you need any help?" Zoey asked.

"No, just give me a minute. I need to use the bathroom. Ladies, feel free to grab whatever you want from that table behind you."

Zoey looked at the table in question that had been set up in a corner. There were hors d'oeuvres in covered trays, juice, and water. Zoey headed over and grabbed some pretzel bites, beef-vegetable rolls, and avocado bruschetta. She'd had breakfast, but she was already hungry. The ladies also grabbed some food as well.

"This wedding planning involves so many moving parts," Dana said. "Thank goodness I only plan to get married once."

Jasmine arched an eyebrow. "No marriage renewal ceremony? It's the in-thing now."

"It's not really my style," Dana responded. "I can't imagine Josh caring about it either."

"Are we really talking about the same Josh?" Alicia said. "The social butterfly? Just make sure he doesn't hear about a renewal ceremony, otherwise you'd have over five hundred people show up to your house for it!"

They all laughed at the thought.

"So Zoey, are you single?" Jasmine asked.

"Oh my goodness, you don't give up, do you?" Alicia said.

Zoey chuckled. "It's not a mystery. Yes, I'm single."

"Hmmm," Jasmine said. "Now, I wonder why Becca was being super protective?" Then her face brightened like she'd had a light bulb moment. "Wait! Does one of Max's brothers like you?"

Zoey's ears grew warm, but she managed to maintain a calm demeanor. She wasn't prepared to talk about Dex. "I have no idea," she said.

"I don't think I'm wrong though," Jasmine murmured to herself.

"Let it go, Jasmine," Alicia said. "This might be uncomfortable for Zoey."

"Sorry," Jasmine said in a contrite voice.

"No worries," Zoey said. "So are you all done with your residencies?"

"In a few weeks, and then we're free," Alicia responded. "That was one of the reasons we moved our wedding from the spring to summer. That and Jasmine needed time to recover from her surgery."

"Is everything alright, Jasmine?" Zoey asked.

Jasmine gave her a small smile. "Just a double mastectomy for breast cancer."

Zoey froze, the pretzel she'd been about to bite left hanging in mid-air. That was the last thing she'd expected to hear. How did Jasmine manage to be so cheerful? Zoey couldn't imagine how she would feel if she lost her breasts.

"It's fine," Jasmine continued. "I've had months to come to terms with the loss. Having the love and support of my fiancé David, my family, and my friends, and a trust in God has been instrumental in getting through it."

"Wow, you're a strong woman," Zoey said.

Jasmine smiled. "I imagine you'd be able to pull through it if you faced the same challenge."

"Okay, I'm back," Becca said as she reentered the room. "What did I miss?"

A ringtone pierced the air at that moment. Becca pulled out her phone from her pocket and checked the screen. "It's Maggie," she said. She strode over and settled into her seat. "I'm going to put her on speakerphone." She pressed a button and placed the phone on the coffee table. "Hello, Maggie. I have you on speakerphone. Alicia, Dana, and Jasmine are here, along with a new friend of mine, Zoey."

"Hi, ladies!" Maggie said in a sweet voice from the other end of the line. "Nice to meet you, Zoey." So this was Dex's foster mom.

"Hello, Maggie!" Dana, Alicia, and Jasmine said at the same time.

"Nice to meet you too," Zoey chimed in.

"How's the honeymoon?" Jasmine asked.

"It's been wonderful. Going to new places, trying exotic food, and meeting new people."

"And with Dr. Taylor by your side," Jasmine said.

"Exactly. We're making new memories together. Oh, he just walked in. Let me get him to say hello." There was a brief noise in the background.

"Hello, ladies," a masculine voice said.

"Hello, Dr. Taylor!" Dana said. The other ladies said their greetings as well.

He chuckled. "It's Peter, please. I've already gotten enough 'Dr. Taylor' at the hospital to last me a lifetime."

"We can't help it, Dr. Taylor," Dana said. "It's like meeting medical royalty."

Zoey understood the feeling. She'd been shocked too when Max had told her Dr. Taylor was a member of his family.

"So, Becca, I saw your missed calls," Maggie said. "Is everything all right?"

"I'll leave you ladies to your discussion," Dr. Taylor said.

"No, please stay," Becca said. "You need to hear this as well."

"Is something wrong?" Maggie asked with concern.

"Promise me you won't come running back home after I tell you," Becca said.

"What is it? You're scaring me."

"You have to promise me first."

"Okay, I promise."

"I had to see the doctor yesterday," Becca said. "I'd been experiencing some memory loss."

"Oh my goodness," Maggie said. "Please tell me there's nothing wrong. You're too young to experience dementia."

"They ran some tests. Turns out I'm pregnant. It was early pregnancy brain."

"What?" the ladies screamed.

"Thank you, God!" Maggie burst into tears.

"Maggie, are you okay?" Becca said.

"I'm fine. That's what you get for scaring an old woman. My heart dropped!"

"I'm sorry."

"Congratulations," Dr. Taylor said. "That's wonderful news."

"I have another grandchild on the way. Oh my goodness," Maggie said. "When are you due?"

"I'll find out later today."

"I need to come home. Peter, you need to book the next flight back."

"Remember you promised, Maggie," Becca said.

"I'm fine now, and I'll still have some ways to go by the time you're done with your honeymoon."

"But what about Chloe? You'll need someone to take care of Chloe while you get enough rest during the pregnancy. I'm sure your doctors will expect you to do the same."

"Don't worry. Max, Dex, and Jax are on top of it, and it's the early days yet. But I promise you I'll rest and take it easy whenever I need to."

"This is such wonderful news. Becca, thank you for making me happy today."

"My pleasure. Let me leave you guys to it."

"Alright," Maggie said. "I'll call you every morning just to make sure you're okay."

"I look forward to it."

"Becca, congrats again," Dr. Taylor said. "Take good care of yourself, okay?"

"I will. Bye."

"Bye," Maggie said. The call disconnected.

Jasmine pounced on Becca. "Congrats! Why didn't you tell me?"

"I wanted Maggie to know first," Becca replied.

"Does Mom know?"

"I called her this morning but asked her to keep it a secret from you. I wanted to break the news to you myself."

"Wow, Aunt Becca," Dana said. "No wonder you're glowing."

"Congrats!" Alicia said. "How are you feeling?"

"I feel good, except I get more tired easily, and then there's the pregnancy brain. I didn't have it with Chloe. That was probably why I didn't recognize it for what it was."

"Maybe it's a boy," Jasmine mused.

"If it is, Willow gets first dibs," Alicia said.

"Willow is Alicia's daughter," Becca whispered to Zoey.

Dana chuckled. "Willow will practically be like a cougar to him."

"Okay, if it's a girl, Blake Junior will get first dibs," Alicia said.

"Blake Junior? Who's that?" Dana said.

"The son Blake and I will have," Alicia said matter-of-factly.

Zoey and everyone else burst into laughter.

"Oh my goodness, Alicia, you're going bonkers," Jasmine said.

Dana wiped the tears from her eyes. "I can't believe Blake Junior, who doesn't yet exist, already has a wife picked out."

"Who can resist those green eyes that run in your family?" Alicia said to Becca.

"You know he or she might end up with blue eyes like Max," Jasmine said.

"Max already donated one pair to Chloe," Alicia insisted. "It's Becca's turn now."

"Did you put something in the water?" Jasmine said to Becca. "Or …wait!" She turned to Alicia. "Do you also have preggy brain?"

"Oh, buzz off!" Alicia said.

Zoey chuckled. These ladies were hilarious. They could keep her entertained all day. She wished she could stay longer, but she guessed Dex might be reaching out sometime soon.

Her phone vibrated. She checked the screen and saw a text from Dex. He was on his way.

She turned to Becca. "Where's the bathroom?"

"Three doors down on the left."

"Thanks." She grabbed her purse and left the room. Zoey found the bathroom easily and was all done with retouching her makeup a few minutes later. She exited and headed back to Becca's office.

"Hi, Zoey," the now familiar voice said, causing the butterflies to come alive in her stomach.

Zoey turned to see Dex looking like the tall drink of water she needed. He was in an army-green Henley over a pair of dark jeans. Some rad-looking cowboy boots graced his feet. "Hi," she said with a smile.

"You look wonderful," he said, his eyes appraising the sky-blue summer dress she'd worn with her own cowboy boots.

"Thank you. You don't look too shabby yourself."

Dex chuckled, the butterflies in Zoey's belly fluttering some more at the sound. This guy had no idea how dangerous his voice was.

"Are you ready?" he asked.

"Give me a few minutes to say goodbye."

"Okay, I'll be in the kitchen," he said.

Zoey reentered the office and strode over to where Becca sat. "I have to go," she said.

"I hope we didn't bore you," Jasmine said.

Zoey chuckled. "I doubt that's possible."

"We aren't always like this," Dana said. *Right.* Zoey would believe it when she saw it.

"Let me see you off," Becca said.

"There's no need."

"Oh … okay."

"I'll talk to you later. It was nice meeting you, ladies. Bye."

"Bye," they said in unison.

Zoey turned, headed to the door, and opened it.

"Zoey?"

Zoey turned at Becca's voice. "Yes?"

"Please extend my regards to Dex," Becca said as her eyes scanned her list.

"I knew it!" Jasmine said. "See, I was right. One of Max's brothers likes you."

Becca gave her a sharp glance. "Jasmine—"

"Alright. I won't say anything else."

Zoey chuckled and closed the door. *Becca, Becca.* She always knew how to say the unexpected. She'd probably heard Dex's voice outside the door.

She'd enjoyed her time with Becca, Alicia, Jasmine, and Dana, but now she was craving a little bit more peace and quiet.

The type she was hoping being around Dex, and maybe the horses, would bring.

Zoey's heart beat faster. Because it could very well end up the opposite.

Zoey followed Dex out the front door and into the fresh air. Fortunately, the afternoon sun wasn't as hot as she'd expected, and she'd applied some sunscreen before coming to the ranch.

"I hope you don't mind walking over," he said. "The horse barn isn't far away."

"That works for me," she said. "It'll give me a chance to burn off all this rich food I've been consuming since I came into town."

"I doubt you need to. You look great as you are," he said.

Zoey's face grew warm. "Why, thank you."

Dex led her along the side of the house until they were walking down a paved path in the direction of a large building with sliding doors. Zoey noticed he'd slowed his strides to match hers.

Nice. She liked when a man was considerate of who he was walking with. It was one of her pet peeves and a better metric—as far as she was concerned—of how a man truly felt about a woman than what he professed to her.

As they neared, Zoey guessed the building was the horse barn. It looked like it had either been newly constructed or undergone some recent renovation with its fresh coat of paint that appeared to have never experienced the harsh winter they'd left behind a few months ago.

"Have you been around horses before?" Dex asked.

"Yes," she said quietly. She remembered how wonderful it had been all those years ago. Well, before the incident. "But that was a long time ago."

They reached the large barn. He unlocked the sliding doors and pushed a side open. "After you," he said.

Zoey took a deep breath and exhaled. This was it. Time to experience heaven on earth again, or her worst nightmare, depending on how she looked at it. She gave him a small smile and entered, and Dex followed behind.

The familiar smell of sweet hay, sweaty leather, and fresh pine shavings hit her nostrils, and Zoey almost buckled. The memories came rushing back like a whirlwind, and she fought the urge to turn and run away. Instead, she took a deep breath and forced herself to look around.

The barn was one of the best she'd seen— spacious with rows and rows of horse stalls laid out in what looked like an upgraded version of the European-style stalls she'd seen before.

Each horse stall had the hinged European-style door made of steel and wood. The lower section was mostly wood framed in steel while the upper section had bars molded into a V, which gave easy access to the horses without entering the stall. The interior looked clean and pristine, not what she'd expect from a barn that had been in use for a while. There was a second-level hay loft, and freshly-packed hay bales filled the space.

"This looks really nice," she said in a steady voice, even though her pulse was still racing.

"Thank you. It's been newly renovated. We had a fire here a couple of months ago, so we used it as an opportunity to upgrade the space."

"Oh, no! Hope everyone was okay."

"Yes. It was by God's grace we didn't lose anyone, people or horses. Okay, this way."

He led her down the cobblestone aisle. Most of the stalls were occupied, and some of the horses trotted to their door in hopes of a treat. Zoey felt like reaching out to them and patting them on the neck, but something held her back. It was like a barrier she couldn't, and was afraid to, break. She also reasoned with herself that it was best to follow Dex's lead, since each horse had its own temperament.

"We'll start at this end," Dex said.

The last two stalls appeared larger than the others. Dex headed to the one on Zoey's left. She watched as a beautiful dark thoroughbred mare rose from where she'd lain and ambled to the stall door.

Zoey fought both the attraction and fear she felt and instead stayed rooted in her spot.

Dex reached out and rubbed the horse's neck. "You feeling better, girl?"

The horse nuzzled her nose against Dex's shirt in response.

Dex chuckled. "Bella, if you're looking for a treat, that means you're definitely better." He pulled out some baby carrots from his pocket, laid them on his palm, and offered them to her. The horse quickly chomped them down.

Zoey watched, transfixed. She loved how gentle he was with the horse, speaking to her in a soothing tone even as he continued to rub her down.

A pang of hurt flashed through Zoey's heart. There was a time she'd done things like this every day, thinking it would last forever, instead it had ended in despair and misery.

"Do you want to … Are you okay?" Dex asked, his voice bringing Zoey back to the present.

"Oh … I'm fine," she said weakly. She felt like she'd run a marathon just revisiting the memories.

"Are you sure? You look a little pale." He left the horse's side and came over to where she stood.

Even though they weren't touching, his nearness warmed and stabilized her, and Zoey could feel her strength returning. "I just need a moment," she said softly.

"We can go if you like, if this is too much," Dex said, concern written all over his face. "I can get one of the ranch hands to feed the horses."

"No, it's fine," Zoey said. "I feel better now. Let's go on."

He studied her face for a moment. "Okay," he said finally. "Would you like to meet Bella?"

"Sure." She had to try, even though her legs felt as heavy as lead as Dex led her to the horse.

"Bella, meet Zoey. She's a friend of mine and a nice lady," Dex said.

Bella's head swung in Zoey's direction.

Zoey swallowed, not knowing what to expect. But the eyes that met hers seemed to look through her into her soul like she understood, letting her know it was okay. That everything was okay.

Tears rose unbidden to Zoey's eyes as she took one tentative step closer, and then another, until she was right next to Bella. She could see the acceptance and understanding in Bella's eyes as she waited.

Zoey closed her eyes and took a calming breath. She wasn't sure how her next action would be received, but she had to do it. Every cell in her yearned to do it. She opened her eyes, leaned forward slowly, little by little, her heart beating loudly in her chest until she laid her head softly against Bella's neck. The heat from Bella enveloped her, warming her and bringing every trepidation and fear that had stood like a barricade between Zoey and a time like this crashing down.

Bella nuzzled her nose against Zoey's neck, and her shoulders relaxed. It was like the fractured pieces of her, the areas she'd wrapped up and hidden within herself, were now loosened, with the fissures beginning to heal together again.

Zoey didn't know she'd been crying until she felt the silent tears roll down her cheeks. She buried her face further into Bella and then wrapped her arms around her neck. Yet Bella stayed and didn't move away.

The world stood still for a few minutes, that part of her healing and becoming whole again, while the tears flowed, and then finally stopped. Then Zoey remembered where she was and who she was with. "Thank you," she whispered softly to Bella.

Bella neighed in return as if she understood.

But now Zoey had to face Dex. She'd cried in front of him after all. But something told her he would understand.

She let go of Bella's neck and then leaned against the stall, looking out into the aisle and refusing to meet his eyes. "It was twenty-four years ago,'" she said. It seemed like a lifetime ago. "I had just completed my first horse riding competition, and we'd come home. I was so happy. It was my first gold medal ever, and I was proud of my horse. Lily was her name. She was a Marwari—I loved her cute inward-facing ears. She was graceful and gentle. Except when it was game time, and then she would run like wildfire." Zoey chuckled at the memory. "That day was supposed to be the best day of my life, and I was looking forward to the cake my mom had baked. My father offered to brush down Lily, and my mom decided to help him. I headed into the house, had a shower and changed and was just heading downstairs when I heard a scream from outside."

Zoey closed her eyes and took another breath. This was the first time she had talked about that day to anyone. Her father had made her see a child psychologist after the incident, but Zoey had been unable to talk about it. The words had never come. Until now.

She felt rather than saw Dex move closer to her, and then his hand covered hers and held it. The warmth that coursed through her drove back the bile that rose in her throat at the memories. "I rushed out of the house and saw my father cradling my mother in his arms. He'd already called nine-one-one. It turned out Lily had been spooked by a rattlesnake that had hidden in her stall. Lily had unknowingly kicked my mother in the head in her bid to get away."

Tears rose at the back of her eyes and threatened to fall, but Zoey forced them back. She had to continue and face the hardest parts of the memories, otherwise she might never be able to speak about them again. Dex must have felt it because his thumb began to rub the back of her hand, calming and soothing her. "But it was too late. My mom died three hours later in the hospital. What had been the best day of my life was now the worst."

She ran her free hand through her hair. "I don't know how I survived the funeral and the next few weeks. It was like I lived in a haze through it all. I only came to my senses on the day I couldn't find Lily anymore. It turned out my father had sold her. He couldn't stand to look at her. My heart broke that day. I had lost my mom and my best friend. My father got remarried not long after and moved us all to New York. I'd never gone near a horse again since. Until today."

The moments stretched out between them, quiet but pleasant. Zoey never knew such silence could be comforting. Dex didn't need to speak, yet it was clear he understood, and that was enough for her.

Zoey's shoulders relaxed, free of the burden she'd carried around for so long. She could breathe more easily now. Everything around her seemed changed— fresher and brighter as if the cobwebs that had clouded her vision had been cleared away. If this was the only reason she'd come to Dexin Valley, then it'd been worth it.

She turned to Dex. "Thanks for bringing me here

and letting me meet Bella." Zoey turned and patted her neck. "She's special."

"She is. She's Max's, yet she's everyone's favorite."

"I can see why. Have you ever tried music with the horses?"

"Music? No."

"Lily used to love it. She would swish her tail back and forth in time with the music's beat."

Dex gave her an incredulous look. "You're kidding, right?"

"I'm serious. It used to amuse my mom and me. But do you play music?"

"Used to. Not anymore."

"Why?"

"No time. It can get very busy at the ranch, and it became less of a priority over time."

"That's a pity." Dex gave her a sharp look. "It's sort of my fantasy to have a cowboy strumming his guitar and singing to me with the sunset as a backdrop."

"I hope your wish comes true."

"I hope so too." She flashed him a warm smile.

"You miss her, don't you?" Dex asked.

Zoey knew who he was referring to. Of course she did. Every time she'd done well in school or gotten an award, when she'd had her first period, when she graduated high school and gotten into college, and even when she'd made it into the residency program, she'd missed her mom. Her father had said the perfunctory congratulations, but Zoey knew her mom would have done something special, even if it was just as simple as taking her out for lunch at the mall to celebrate. "I do."

"What about your stepmother?"

"She has her daughter," Zoey replied. But today was a happy day, and she didn't want to think about them, especially *her*.

"I think this might be a good time to attend to the other horses," Dex said as he gestured down the aisle. "What do you think?"

Zoey chuckled. Most of the other horses had poked their heads out of the stalls. It was like she had an audience. "That's a great idea."

Dex let go of her hand and moved to what she assumed was the tack room. His hand had felt warm and safe, and suddenly Zoey felt bereft of it. He soon returned with a manure fork in one gloved hand and a large paper bag in another. "I need to muck her stall," he said. "Why don't you offer the other horses some treats?" He handed the bag over to her. "They won't bite. Well, except for Lexi." He pointed to the opposite stall as he leaned the manure fork against the wall. The horse in question was nowhere to be seen, probably relaxing in her stall and not caring to be bothered.

"You really decided to go with that name?" Zoey said.

He'd headed over to a corner outside the tack room and now came back with a wheelbarrow she hadn't noticed earlier. Dex shrugged. "She seems to like it."

"Alright. I'll head over to the other horses."

"Thank you."

So Zoey went down the line, tentative at first but growing more comfortable with the horses. She took her time in getting to know each one and handed out treats while Dex cleaned the stalls that needed it and made sure each one was stocked with fresh hay. Some horses chomped on their treats and quickly retreated back into their stalls, while others nuzzled her and Zoey played and laughed with them. It felt good, freeing even, to forget about the world outside and just spend her time here with the horses.

Soon, the last horse had been taken care of, the tools had been returned, and they'd washed their hands. Zoey stepped out into the open air. It was now late afternoon, the smell of green grass floating in the fresh breeze.

"Thanks for all your help," Dex said as they began to walk back to the main house.

"It was nothing," Zoey responded. Their shoulders brushed together, and Zoey felt a spark of electricity buzz through her. Zoey glanced at him, but she couldn't tell from his expression if he'd felt it too.

"I know it's way past lunchtime, but would you like something to eat?" Dex asked. "I'm a mean cook and could quickly put something together."

Zoey stifled a yawn. "Some other time," she said. "I think I need a nap more than food." The black limousine was no longer in front of the house, which meant the ladies were gone.

Soon they arrived in front of her car, and Zoey got in. She turned to look at Dex. "I had a good time," she said.

"Me too. Maybe I'll get another chance to take you somewhere that doesn't involve mucking a stall."

Zoey laughed. "I'll hold you to it."

"Do you mind if I call on you sometime? Maybe soon?"

Smooth. "Not at all."

The smile on his face was reward enough. "Have

a good evening, Zoey," he said. She loved the way her name sounded on his lips.

"You too." Zoey pulled out of the parking spot and gave him a wave, which he returned.

But she could still see him in the rearview mirror, standing in the spot where she'd left him.

CHAPTER 17

*D*ex showered and then made a quick sandwich for a late lunch. He carried his plate and drink to his back porch where he had a great view of the mountains.

What had happened this afternoon had been so unexpected, yet Dex was glad he'd been there to comfort Zoey in the way she'd needed. He'd had no idea she'd been carrying such a heavy burden, and it felt good that she'd trusted him enough to share it with him.

But he'd been surprised by her love for horses. Dex had thought she was a city lady through and through. That just went to reinforce that he should never judge a book by its cover.

But did this mean there was a possibility she

would love living on the ranch? Dex didn't want to get his hopes up—loving horses was different from living and breathing ranch life. But he couldn't help holding onto the possibility that there was a chance. No one had thought Becca would adapt to ranch life, and yet she had. Maybe he needed to believe that it was also possible for Zoey to do the same.

Dex took a sip of his drink. But that wasn't all that mattered. He needed to get to know Zoey more, though he'd liked what he'd discovered so far. What if they were only meant to be friends and nothing more? Then again, his skin buzzed wherever it met hers, and her nearness tended to unravel him. It had taken everything in him not to wrap her in his arms when she'd started sobbing.

And there was still the matter of her job. What if she didn't like Dexin Valley enough to stay and work here? Sure, she'd had the interview with Max, but that didn't mean anything. What if she didn't get the job—though he doubted that from what Max had mentioned in passing about Zoey—or decided not to take the job offer? Dex didn't know enough of the medical world to be able to tell the value of what Max was offering her.

Finally, Zoey was only here on vacation and would probably return soon. Dex had no idea how much longer she'd be around. What if he opened his heart, and then she left? He'd be devastated.

Dex needed to guard his heart. Sure, he would continue to get to know her better, but he would do so as a friend and nothing more.

It was best not to get his hopes up.

Though his heart seemed disappointed at the thought.

CHAPTER 18

Zoey stretched as she woke up from her nap. She'd arrived back to the B&B to see Miss Prissy had left a plate of food for her in her room, so she'd quickly eaten and washed up before falling into bed.

Now she felt refreshed, her body lighter. She'd left her curtains open, and she could see the sun had set, the darkness of the streets only punctuated by the streetlights or a passing vehicle.

Zoey yawned. She had no plans to go out tonight. This was one of those evenings where reading a book in bed was all she craved.

Her phone rang at that moment, and Zoey picked it up from the bedside table and scanned the screen. It was her friend, Tara. "Hey," she said as she sat up.

"Hey, you. Did you decide to drop off the face of the planet or what?"

The corners of Zoey's lips turned up in a smile. Tara could be so dramatic. "I've been right here."

"Exactly. And you never bothered to call and give me all the details."

"About what? The interview? It's like every other one we've had."

"I bet it wasn't. It was at a ranch, right?"

"Yes. But Dr. Dexin is a doctor, so the interview was just like any other."

"And did you meet any hot cowboys?"

Zoey hesitated for a moment as she recalled Dex. Yes, he definitely fell in that category with his broad shoulders, his lean build, and warm brown eyes. "What do you mean?" she said.

Tara shrieked. "You met one, didn't you?"

Zoey held her phone away from her ear for a few seconds. "Hey, do you want to damage my eardrums?" she asked as she returned to the call. "I have no plans to start wearing hearing aids at this age."

"Don't change the subject. Spill. Quick."

Zoey told her about Dex, how she'd met him, and the other encounters they'd had.

"You like him, don't you?" Tara said once Zoey had finished.

"Why do you say that?"

"I can hear it in your voice. You're excited about him."

"It doesn't mean anything."

"Yes, it does."

"Really?"

"Yes. In fact, I don't think I've ever heard you talk about anyone like that. Not even the boy in the shoebox photo. What was his name again?"

"Zach."

"Yes, Zach. You obviously like Dex more than you liked him."

Zach had been a childhood crush, in a chapter of Zoey's life that was closed forever. It was like comparing apples to oranges. "I don't know. I think we're just getting to know each other as friends."

"I think you want him to be more than a friend," Tara said.

Zoey ran a hand through her hair. "I don't know. You know how I feel about relationships. I also have work to think of. Even though the job here sounds promising, there's no guarantee I'll get it. Even if I do, I'm not sure what my decision would be. I think I'd prefer to work in an established hospital and learn from others more experienced than I am at this stage in my career, which probably means living in the city. I can't imagine Dex agreeing to that when the nearest city hospital is over two hours away. He loves the ranch, and I think that's important to him. Besides, this was supposed to be a short visit."

"You're getting ahead of yourself," Tara said. "I think it's more important to focus on discovering what your hearts feel about each other. Then you can cross that bridge when you get to it."

"I'm not sure I can do that. I don't need any more heartbreaks in my life."

"Okay. Why don't you let your heart lead the way for now in this friendship, and then you can reevaluate later? Maybe start off by going out on a real date?"

"After the disastrous one we had? I don't think so. Dex is also an introvert."

"Then you make the move. There's no rule that says the man has to do so first. And you don't need to attach the 'date' label to it as long as it achieves its aim."

True. "Okay, I'll try," Zoey said. "But only as a friend."

"If that's what you choose to call it. At least the she-devil—"

"No, we can't talk about her," Zoey said abruptly. *She* had no place in this conversation.

"I'm sorry. I shouldn't have brought her up. But you have to keep me updated on how things go with the hunk. I want all the details."

"We'll see."

"Hey, you can't start holding out on me now!" Zoey heard some shuffling in the background. "I have to go."

"Where are you off to?"

"I have a dinner date. You're not the only one having some fun."

"Anyone I know?"

"Don't worry. It's a group date thingy with Larry." Larry was one of Tara's childhood friends.

"Okay. Enjoy your date."

"I will. Talk to you later. Bye."

"Bye." The call ended.

Zoey dropped her phone beside her and laid back on the bed. Tara's advice made sense. Maybe she was getting ahead of herself. They could explore what they had as friends without the added pressure of assigning labels to it. Besides, there were so many things that were up in the air—one of which was a job offer from Dr. Dexin. If she didn't get the job, then everything else was a moot point. As much as she liked Dex and wished to know more about him, she couldn't drop everything and mess up her future, even for him.

Her phone beeped, signaling an email alert. Zoey lifted her phone and swiped the screen.

She sprang up, her eyes widening as she read the email.

Zoey had just received a formal job offer from the Dexin ER Center.

But she only had two weeks to accept or reject the offer. It wasn't enough time, considering she hadn't heard back from the other hospitals.

Zoey fell back on her bed. What was she going to do now?

CHAPTER 19

Zoey had spent the night tossing and turning. The email had derailed any reading plans she'd had. Instead, she'd spent the rest of the evening considering her options, after she'd forwarded the contract to her lawyer, who specialized in physician contracts and had been a big help during her negotiations so far. But now it was already noon, and she'd come no closer to a decision.

Two weeks was much shorter than she'd expected and was very different from the time she'd spent so far negotiating with the other hospitals. The other hospitals hadn't gotten back to her on the counteroffers she'd made, yet the offer from Dexin ER Center, at first glance, already had most of the terms she'd wanted included in the contract.

It was as if Dr. Dexin had read her heart and anticipated most of her needs. That could only have been possible from paying attention to what most new attendings were requesting now. *Smart man.* Also, their base pay was higher than what she'd been offered at the other hospitals. The contract included automatic renegotiations of terms after one year as well. That had been a surprise to Zoey but a much-welcomed clause. None of the other hospitals had offered that.

But she was still worried that she might not get the exposure she needed. Zoey had to be careful not to stifle her career or her growth opportunities. Of course, she planned to make a counteroffer that would allow her to work a few months per year at Dexington Medical to compensate for that, but she wasn't sure how well it would be received, or if it would be accepted. And she still had her concerns about being young and single in a town that was more suitable for married folks.

Then there was Dex in all of this.

Ugh. She didn't know what to think. Maybe going outside and getting some fresh air would help.

Zoey brushed her hair, put on some light makeup, donned a long T-shirt knotted at one side with a pair of slim-fitted jeans, and grabbed her sunglasses.

She'd made her way to the door when she turned back and picked up the keys to her car. Maybe a drive might be better.

She headed down the stairs and soon reached the foyer. The place was quiet save for the humming sound of the HVAC in the background. Zoey noticed the main door had been propped open. She could see Connie was outside, lifting some boxes into the trunk of her car, which was parked curbside.

"Hello, Zoey."

Zoey turned to see Miss Prissy. She was dressed in an apron over a flowery blouse and a pair of jeans.

"Good day, Miss Prissy," Zoey said. She liked her despite how fierce her lips were in spreading rumors.

"Just the person I was looking for," Miss Prissy said.

Now why would that be? "Is everything alright?" Zoey asked.

"I wanted to let you know I have your second date all lined up for you."

"Second date?" What was Miss Prissy talking about?

"Yes. You did promise to go on three dates, if I recall."

Zoey wasn't interested in any more dates, but she wasn't exactly dating Dex, so what excuse could she give to decline them? Even if she was dating Dex, there was no way she was telling Miss Prissy *that*. It would be equivalent to standing on the rooftop and blaring the news to everyone with a megaphone. And Zoey had to keep her word—Miss Prissy had certainly done her part in providing the tasty meals.

"Okay, I'll go on the second date."

"Wonderful," Miss Prissy said. Then she seemed to look beyond Zoey. "Isn't that Dex Dexin headed down the stairs?"

Zoey turned, and sure enough, it was Dex hurrying down the stairs like his pants were on fire. What was he doing here? He seemed to be holding something in his hands.

Zoey gasped as she realized what had just happened.

CHAPTER 20

$\mathcal{D}$ex had whistled all morning even as he went through his chores. The ranch hands had commented on how cheery he'd sounded, and even Fred, the ranch manager, had teased him mercilessly about it. But it hadn't bothered Dex—nothing could penetrate his armor of happiness.

Becca had noticed but said nothing. She'd looked a bit tired, and Dex guessed that the pregnancy was still getting to her. So when she'd wanted to head into town to give Zoey some Fijian sweets that Maggie had sent, Dex had offered to help. Of course, it didn't have anything to do with the fact that he'd wanted to see Zoey again.

Dex parked his car in the only available parking spot across the street, crossed over, and made his way up the stairs of Miss Prissy's B&B with the box of sweets in hand. Everyone at the house had enjoyed some of the Fijian dried fruits, and Dex was confident Zoey would love them too.

Then he heard voices, one in particular that he was drawn to like a moth to a flame.

Dex halted. The door was propped open, and Zoey's voice carried to where he stood.

"Okay, I'll go on the second date," she said.

Dex's heart skipped a beat, and the smile on his face froze. Zoey was going on a second date? Sure, they weren't dating officially, but she had to be aware that he was interested in her. He'd thought she felt the same way about him. Dex had assumed this period was about taking it slow and getting to know each other before committing to dating. Had he been mistaken?

But he couldn't stay and find out—letting her see him now would be humiliating. She'd done nothing wrong, yet it still hurt. He couldn't allow her to see how much it did.

Dex bounded down the stairs and hurried to his car.

He drove away as fast as possible.

Zoey's pulse raced as she thought about what to do. Running after Dex was not an option, since Miss Prissy was as perceptive as could be and would immediately put two and two together. Yet she couldn't let him leave like that without explaining what he'd just overheard. So Zoey said her goodbyes to Miss Prissy and strode back to her room to pick up her purse.

By the time she'd made her way back downstairs, Miss Prissy was nowhere to be found. Zoey left quickly and hurried down the sidewalk and around the block until she reached the lot where she'd parked her car.

She drove as fast as she could without breaking the speed limit. Soon she arrived at the ranch and ran into Becca coming from the barn just as she was exiting her car.

"Hello, Zoey," Becca said.

"Hey, Becca. Now what would a pregnant woman such as yourself be doing in a horse barn?" she asked.

Becca laughed. "No need to worry. I've done nothing dangerous except feed Bella some apple slices."

"How is she?"

"She's good. You've met her?"

"Yes, I have. Dex introduced her to me yesterday. Do you happen to know where he might be?"

"What happened to him? He was chipper just a while ago, but now seemed dejected for some reason. He was so out of it he didn't even react when I said I was going to see Bella. That's unusual for him."

Zoey's heart sank. This was even worse than she'd thought. "I'm sure it's nothing. But I need to speak with him. He stopped by the B&B and left so quickly we didn't get a chance to connect."

"Okay. He'll probably be in his workshop. You see that road that branches off the driveway on the right side of the house?"

Zoey looked to where Becca was pointing, and sure enough, there was a road there. "Yes."

"Follow it and you'll eventually see a log house

similar to this one with a dark blue door at its entrance. That's his house. The workshop, where he probably is, has its own entrance on the side. It's best if you take your car."

"Thank you," she said to Becca.

"My pleasure," Becca replied. "Just get him out of that funk."

"I'll try."

"Good."

Zoey left Becca there, headed back to her car, and found her way to the side road. She followed it past some more manicured lawns until she spotted the beautiful house with the dark blue door, built in a ranch-style design. But its surrounding gardens had more herbs and vegetables—it seemed Dex had a green thumb.

She parked in front of the house and then walked round to the side until she found the workshop entrance Becca had described. She climbed its steps and searched for a bell, but there was none. Zoey knocked on the door.

There was no response.

After she knocked again and nothing happened, she tried the knob.

The door swung open.

Zoey stepped in and closed the door behind her.

The space was somewhat dark—the farmhouse shutters on the windows were closed—but Zoey's eyes soon adjusted to it. It seemed like a receiving area with a couple leather-backed chairs and a coffee table with magazines on one side and what looked like a mini kitchen on the other side. There was an open archway that connected the receiving room to an inner area.

Zoey made her way through it and entered into the largest studio she'd ever seen. She didn't know much about leatherworking, but she'd seen a few online videos in passing, and this seemed to be on a much grander scale.

The workshop was massive with large windows on either side. It had the largest table Zoey had ever seen in its center, the wood grains very visible on its surface and twin lamps hanging down from the ceiling over it. A long counter ran along the back wall and had different types of machines resting on its surface. There were racks on the wall above the counter which contained different types of leathers sorted by color, texture, and size. Another section of the wall featured all sorts of instruments, including various types of hammers and mallets bracketed onto it. A wooden storage solution covered another area, each drawer clearly labeled with its contents. The strong smell of leather filled the air.

Zoey could see a figure on a stool near the windows on the left hunched over something with an adjustable lamp at his elbow. She moved closer and realized there was a wooden contraption positioned in front of him which held a piece of leather in its jaws. Dex was pushing in and pulling out a set of large needles along with what looked like thick thread through the piece of leather.

"Dex?" she said.

He carefully dropped the needles he was holding and pushed the lamp away toward the wall. Then he turned and faced her. "Zoey," he replied coolly, his eyes assessing hers.

Zoey didn't know where to begin—might as well jump right into it. "Did you come to see me at the B&B?"

"Why don't you take a seat first?" he said. He pulled out another stool and positioned it in front of her.

Zoey sat down. If she leaned forward a little, their knees would practically be touching.

"Yes, I came to see you," he said quietly.

"So why did you leave?" she asked softly.

He was silent for a moment. Then he ran a hand

through his hair. Dex had no idea how endearing the action was. Then he gazed into her eyes. "I overheard what you said."

"About the date?"

"Yes."

"Dex, I wasn't interested in going on one, but I had no way to refuse her. I'd given Miss Prissy my word that I would go on three dates in exchange for free lunch and dinner, and she has kept her end of the bargain. The only way she'd let me out of it was if I was dating someone, which I'm not. Or am I? You tell me, Dex."

Dex's shoulders sagged. "No, we're not, and that's probably why it hurt," he said honestly. "But I'd like us to be."

A smile tugged at the corners of Zoey's lips. The thought of dating Dex wasn't as scary as she'd imagined. "Are you asking me out?"

He pinched the bridge of his nose and then looked her straight in the eye. "I don't know how this will work, given that you're only here on vacation, but yes, I'd like to date you, Zoey."

Zoey's breath quickened. "Why?"

"I like you. I really like you. You're down-to-earth and funny and beautiful." Zoey's face warmed at his words. "And I'd like to get to know you better, exclusively."

Zoey laughed. "Did you have to use that word at the end?"

Dex chuckled. "I figured I'd better make it clear, with Miss Prissy on you and all. So what do you say?"

Zoey hadn't bargained for a relationship. But even though everything seemed up in the air and relationships still scared her, a part of her wanted this with him. Tara was right. She should let go and just see how this would play out. "Yes, I'll date you," she replied.

"Woohoo!" Dex lifted her off the stool and twirled her around. "Thank you!"

Zoey chuckled. "Put me down, you big oaf."

Dex placed her gently on her feet like she was a delicate treasure, but he kept his arms wrapped around her and stared into her eyes, right into her soul.

Zoey's heart began to beat faster as electricity charged in the air between them. She couldn't have looked away even if she wanted to. Her fingers itched to touch his face, so she reached out and brushed his cheek, grazing those solid masculine lines she'd never get tired of.

Dex's breath hitched, and he leaned closer, his eyes searching hers, waiting, hoping. Soft hints of his fresh scent and minty breath enveloped her, warming and drawing her in.

The butterflies in Zoey's stomach began to flutter. She wasn't sure what Dex planned to do, but she wanted to kiss him, so she stood on tiptoe. It seemed it was all the invitation Dex needed, because his hand cupped the back of her head, his touch sending sparks through her skin.

Then he leaned forward and kissed her.

It was gentle at first, a tender kiss that sent the butterflies in her belly into overdrive. His lips were soft, sweeter than she'd imagined, and she wanted more.

Zoey wrapped her arms around his neck and drew him closer. Dex deepened the kiss, driving away all her doubt and hesitation and replacing it with all the assurance and comfort she needed.

The butterflies in her stomach went crazy. It was like the rest of the world fell away, and now they were the only two people that existed, the kiss flooding her body with warmth, hope, and happiness. When they came up for air, Dex held her in his arms like she was the most precious thing in the world.

Zoey nestled deeper into them, wanting to stay there forever.

She had no idea how the relationship would work out, but being here in his arms, in this moment, felt right.

And not even a second blind date courtesy of Miss Prissy could change that.

Zoey finally broke away from Dex's arms and walked over to see what he'd been working on.

"What is this?" she asked, staring at the awkward piece of leather.

"Just some design ideas I had for a pair of boots. Not sure if it will work out, but there's no harm in trying."

Zoey studied the piece. "I'm not sure how this would turn into a pair of boots, but I like the stitching pattern you've got going on."

"Thank you."

Then she noticed multiple pairs of boots lined up in rows across one wall. They had a high-end look to them—as if they would go for hundreds or thousands at a store. "What are these boots?" she asked, pointing at them.

"I made those."

Zoey's mouth hung open. "You did? Dex, these look so good. I can totally see them at home in a high-end store."

"Thank you."

"I mean it, Dex. These are really good."

Then Zoey noticed some papers on the floor that might have fallen off the desk in the corner. She bent and picked them up. They looked like application forms.

"Oh, those are for something I'm thinking of applying for." Dex took the forms from her.

"Does it have anything to do with bootmaking?" Zoey asked.

"Yes. It's a mentee opportunity with some top masters in the field."

"Have you applied already?"

"Not yet."

"Why ever not?"

"I don't know. These guys have very high standards. I'm not sure if my work is good enough."

Zoey walked over to Dex and wrapped her arms around his waist. "Dex, you should apply."

"You think so?"

"I know so. Your work is exquisite and deserves to be seen."

"Really?"

"Really. So what do you need to apply?"

"I need to fill out the electronic version of the form and attach some photos of my work. I also get the chance to add any extra stuff I believe would help my application."

"You should totally do a video."

Dex shook his head. "I'm sure I'd look terrible."

"Oh no you won't. I only worry that someone else might fall in love with you."

Dex chuckled and gave her a kiss on the forehead. "You're good for my ego."

"So what do you say, cowboy? Should we get the show on the road?"

"Sure."

"Great. Where's the camera? I'm a mean photographer when I want to be."

Dex reached into a cabinet, pulled out his camera, and handed it to her.

"Why don't you work on those forms?" Zoey said. "I'll take pictures of your boots."

"On it."

Zoey spent the next twenty minutes capturing the highlights of Dex's boots in the best possible light. She'd worked the odd job at a fashion magazine while in college, so she knew the basics. By the time she was done, Dex had finished with the forms. That left only the video.

"Dex, I think you should continue working on that piece of leather. Then I'll swing in and you'll look up and introduce yourself, then explain what you're working on, why you love making boots, and what you hope to get from the mentoring program. What do you think?"

"Sounds like a better idea than I could come up with."

"Great. Why don't you get set up, and then I'll start filming?"

Zoey watched as Dex got back to the leather he was working on and soon got lost in it. She took a wide shot of the studio and then honed in on Dex, tapping his arm lightly to get his attention. Dex looked up with a smile and executed perfectly what Zoey had suggested. He was a natural at it and didn't even know it! She'd thought they might end up having to do multiple takes, but one shot, and they were all done.

She shut off the camera and gave him a high-five. "You're so good at this."

"Thank goodness. I wasn't sure if I'd survive another take."

"It was perfect. You were perfect." Zoey showed

him what she'd filmed and the pictures she'd taken.

"Zoey, you're a genius," he said. Zoey's face warmed. "These are really, really good. If you ever decide to hang up your stethoscope, know you have a second career in photography."

"Hmmm. I've never thought about it, but maybe I should pick it up as a hobby."

"You should. These are really good."

"Okay. Why don't we transfer them to your computer and send them in?"

Dex moved the pictures and video over, attached them to the application, and clicked the 'submit' button. They watched as the email disappeared into cyberspace and a confirmation message appeared on the screen.

Dex wrapped his arms around Zoey. "Thank you so much for the encouragement," he said.

"You're very welcome. So what's my reward?"

"What do you want?"

"Well, a kiss might be a good starting point."

"Your wish is my command, Your Highness."

Zoey spent the rest of the afternoon chatting with Dex and then headed back to the B&B. She'd decided it was best to cancel the date—she couldn't go through with it in good faith. It would feel like a deception to lead her blind date on, especially since she was now in a relationship. She would just try and avoid mentioning who she was going out with.

She reached the B&B and let herself in. The foyer was empty, so she headed left toward the kitchen to look for Miss Prissy. The kitchen was usually off-limits to guests, but Miss Prissy had given Zoey permission to use it whenever she liked.

Zoey found her rolling a batch of dough on the butcher block counter which fit the modern country style vibe of the kitchen, with its shiplap walls, apron sinks, shaker style cabinets, all mixed in with stainless steel appliances and modern light fixtures. The room was warm, and the smell of cinnamon and strawberry hung in the air.

Miss Prissy looked up as Zoey entered. "Hello, Zoey," she said. She dropped the pin she was holding and washed her hands at the sink. "I was just looking for you."

"I need to speak with you," Zoey said. "About the date."

Miss Prissy turned and leaned against the sink. Her sharp, intelligent eyes focused on Zoey. "What about?"

"I need to cancel it."

"Why?"

"Well, I now have someone I'm going out with. I don't think it would be fair to whoever my blind date is."

Miss Prissy let out a sigh. "That might be a problem."

"Why?"

"Because the person reached out to me and specifically asked for you. And he should be here soon."

What? "But you didn't say it would be today!"

"His plans changed last minute. I called your number a couple of times to let you know, but I couldn't reach you."

Zoey pulled out her phone and tapped the screen. There was no response. She pressed the power button, and it came on. She must have switched off her phone by mistake.

But who could this person be, and why would he insist on her? "Did he say why? Who is he?"

Miss Prissy picked up a towel and wiped her hands. "I think you should save those questions for him." She looked Zoey up and down. "Or better yet, you should change and get ready."

The doorbell rang at that moment.

"That must be him," Miss Prissy said. "Could you please get the door?"

Zoey sighed. Maybe she should just cancel the date directly with him.

She left the kitchen and headed toward the entrance. She soon reached the door and opened it. The man was standing with his back to her, looking out to the street.

"Hello," she said.

He turned.

Zoey gasped. The last person she'd expected to see was standing in front of her.

A much taller, older version of the person she'd known.

It was the boy from the picture in her shoebox.

CHAPTER 22

Zoey blinked. Was she really seeing who she thought was standing in front of her? "Zach?"

The handsome young man grinned at her. "Zoey. When I heard your name in town, I wasn't sure if it was the same Zoey I knew."

"What are you doing here?"

"I'm supposed to be your date."

Zoey shook her head in disbelief. This couldn't be happening right now.

There was no way she could cancel this date. Zoey and Zach had grown up together, and Zach had been her longtime crush. They'd even made childish commitments that they would marry each other when they grew up. But Zoey's family had moved suddenly, and she hadn't had a chance to say a proper goodbye to him. She couldn't do this to him again. "Come on in," she said.

"Thank you," Zach replied.

She led him to the dining area. "Would you mind waiting for me here for about five minutes?"

"Sure."

"Thanks. Feel free to grab a seat. I'll be right back."

Zoey strode off and hurried up the stairs.

She had to make a call.

She needed to talk to Dex now.

Zoey reached her room and shut its door behind her. Being in a relationship was about being open with one another, and since this was someone who'd been special to her, the date situation had changed. Dex needed to know. She pulled out her phone and called Dex.

"Hey, babe," Dex said in a playful tone. Zoey couldn't help smiling. Then she remembered who she'd left downstairs, and her smile disappeared.

"Hey, Dex."

"Zoey, what's going on? Is something wrong?" he asked.

Dex was as perceptive as ever. "My second date is here."

"Was it supposed to be today?"

"No. But his plans changed, and he spoke to Miss Prissy. She couldn't reach me but gave him the go-ahead anyway."

"Are you okay? You don't have to go if you don't want to."

"It's too late. I've seen him."

"Who is it?"

"It's someone I know. Someone I loved a long time ago." Dex cursed under his breath on the other end of the line. "I don't know what to do."

Dex was silent for a moment. "Do you want to have the date?"

Zoey ran her hand through her head. "I think I need to."

"Do you still love him?" Dex asked.

"It's been a long time, but I don't know," Zoey answered honestly.

"I think you should go on the date."

Zoey's eyes widened. It was the last thing she'd expected to hear. "Why?"

"If you don't, you'll always wonder about him."

"Aren't you mad?"

"I'm not happy about it, but I think this is important for you, so it's fine with me."

"Thank you."

"You're welcome. Call me once you're done, alright?"

"I will."

"Take care, babe."

Zoey grinned. She didn't think she would ever get tired of hearing him call her that. "Okay. Bye."

She dropped the phone beside her.

Now all she had to do was get through the date with Zach.

Zoey quickly changed her top and put on another flowery blouse that was one of her favorites. She pulled her hair into a ponytail, picked up her purse, and then headed downstairs.

Zach looked up as she entered the dining area. He'd picked a book from the bookshelf and had been flipping through it as he leaned against the wall, looking very much like a model on a photography shoot. Zoey knew any woman would be lucky to go out with him.

He straightened. "You look great," he said.

"Thank you," Zoey replied. "Would you like something to drink?"

"I'm good. Thanks," Zach said. He strode over and pulled out a chair for her and then took another for himself.

"So what are you doing in this area?" Zoey asked.

He gave her a warm smile. "I live here."

"Really? I thought …"

"We moved out of Texas a long time ago. My aunt kept talking about this jewel of a place, and my parents caught the traveling bug. So here we are."

"Wow. This is …"

"Unbelievable?"

Zoey chuckled. It seemed their habit of finishing each other's sentences hadn't changed. She'd never thought she'd see him again. "It's good to see you. How many years has it been?"

Zach thought for a minute. "Over twenty?"

"That's a long time." A lot had happened in that period. The boy she'd grown up with and had a crush on had matured into a man. Zoey herself had also changed. "How's your family?"

"They're all good. My parents love working the ranch as usual. Valerie is now a veterinarian." Valerie was Zach's younger sister.

"I'm not surprised. She always did have a way with animals. Saved every hurt critter she ever saw."

"True."

"What about you?"

"I'm a professor of agricultural law at the local college."

"Wow. I'm not surprised though. You were great in debate club."

Zach chuckled. "You haven't changed. What about you?"

"I'm a doctor."

"Really?" He leaned back. "Now why do I recall you being squeamish when Charlie hurt his leg?" Charlie had been the barn cat at Zach's home.

Zoey laughed. "I've overgrown that. I'll have you know that I work in the ER all the time, right in the thick of things."

"It's good to see you again, Zoey."

It was really nice to catch up with Zach. There were so many good memories between them, and she would forever treasure Zach as a friend. But all she could think of was those brown eyes that called to her. Only one person filled her thoughts and her heart. Zoey crossed her legs. "Now about our date."

"You're not single."

Zoey looked at him in surprise. "How did you know?"

"I've seen Dex since I heard about your blind date. He's changed."

Wonders would never cease. "You know him?"

Zach nodded. "I get to see him now and then. He's someone I respect."

"I'm sorry." She felt bad for turning him down, but seeing Zach hadn't changed how she felt about Dex.

"Me too. But I'll see you around? I'm sure my parents would love to see you."

"Maybe sometime," Zoey said. "We should definitely stay in touch."

"We should." They exchanged numbers and then sat in companionable silence for a moment. "What about your dad?" Zach then asked.

"He's good," Zoey responded. "Family is in New York."

"Please send my regards to him."

"I will."

Zach got to his feet. "I won't take up any more of your time."

Zoey rose as well. "It was great seeing you again." She leaned forward and gave Zach a hug.

"Take care of you," she said. It had been their parting mantra.

"Take care of you too," Zach responded. She watched as he left.

It wasn't the way Zoey had planned for her story with Zach to end, but she was glad they'd finally had closure.

Now she could call Dex.

She paused for a moment. No, she had a better idea.

Zoey raced back to her room.

CHAPTER 23

*D*ex paced back and forth in his living room like he was on pins and needles. He'd been restless since he'd received the call from Zoey about her male friend.

He checked the time on his phone. Only thirty minutes since she'd last called. Was she done with her ex? Of course, he could call and find out, but he didn't want to put any pressure on her. It had to be her choice. Zoey had to come to him of her own free will.

But what if it had been a mistake to let her go on the date? This was her old flame for goodness sake, and she'd loved him. What if this date rekindled what they had before, and he lost her?

Dex jumped at the sudden blast of thunder. He

strode to the windows and looked outside. The skies had darkened and soon it began to rain, slowly at first and then a torrential downpour as if foreboding what was about to happen between him and Zoey. It hadn't rained all summer. Why did it have to come down this very evening when he needed to hear from her?

There was a knock on the door. Dex guessed it was Jax, and frankly, he didn't want to see him. All he needed now was a call from Zoey.

The knock persisted. *Aargh.* He didn't need this. Dex strode to the door with the intent to give whoever was on the other side of the door a piece of his mind. He jerked it open, stunned at what he saw.

Zoey stood before him, drenched from head to toe and shivering.

"Come in, come in," he said. Dex hurried her in, not caring she was leaving puddles of water on the floor. The only thing on his mind was getting her dry and out of the cold. "Hold on one second." He rushed into the nearest bathroom, grabbed the first two towels he could find, and raced back to Zoey. He wrapped the first towel around her. "We need to get you out of these clothes," he said. He picked up the second towel to dry her hair.

Zoey grabbed his arm. "Dex, please hold on. I have something to say."

"What if you catch a cold?"

"It doesn't matter. I'd like to say what's on my mind before I lose my nerve."

Dex forced himself to halt, but his pulse raced. What if she was planning to break up with him? "Okay."

"Dex, the date didn't really happen. I only chatted with him."

Dex heart rate increased its pace. "Why?"

"Because of you. I, Zoey Brown, choose you, Dex—"

Dex kissed the rest of her words away. The kiss was the sweetest nectar, full of tenderness and love, and he hoped she understood the message he was communicating from his heart about how precious she was to him. When she wrapped her arms around his neck, Dex almost lost it. He couldn't get enough and deepened the kiss, sharing an avalanche of love and adoration, a language all its own. And Zoey responded in kind.

Soon they broke apart. "Wow," Zoey said.

Dex smiled. "What?"

"You're a good kisser."

"It takes two to kiss, my darling."

Zoey blushed, and Dex's smile broadened. She

looked so cute and endearing. But she was still wet and needed to change before she caught a cold.

"Why don't we get you out of these clothes?" Dex said. He led her to one of the guest rooms and showed her the bathroom. "I'll be right back." He left and soon returned with a clean shirt and a pair of shorts. "Sorry, I don't have any smaller clothes," he said. "You can take a hot shower if you like. Just come out whenever you're done."

"Thank you," she said.

"You're welcome." Dex closed the guest room door behind him and headed to the kitchen. Zoey would need something hot, so he put together some chicken vegetable soup and coffee.

Then Dex sat in the living room and waited for her.

For the woman he was now sure had stolen his heart.

CHAPTER 24

Zoey put on the clothes Dex had brought for her. They were oversized, but she loved the smell of him on them. Fortunately, she'd worn a belt with her jeans, so she used it to hold the shorts up. Zoey carried her wet clothes in her arms and left the guest room.

She found Dex in the living room, switching the channels on the TV from one to the other. He jumped to his feet as soon as he saw her.

"Where's the laundry room?" Zoey asked, gesturing to the clothes in her arms.

"I'll handle it," Dex said, taking them from her. "Why don't you sit down? I'll be right back." He turned and headed down the hall to the left. Zoey had been independent for so long that it was nice having someone take care of her for a change.

She looked around the space. Though it appeared more masculine with its decor of greys and browns, the occasional teal-colored item added a warmth to the space that she appreciated. It boasted an open floor plan layout that included a living room, a dining room, and a spectacular kitchen.

The kitchen was designed for someone who actually knew how to cook, not someone like her that could barely make the occasional sandwich. From what she could see, this area was Dex's pride and joy with its top-of-the-line stainless steel appliances and massive kitchen counter. Zoey loved a man who cooked, and it seemed Dex fit the bill to a tee.

"Are you done admiring the kitchen?" a voice said from behind her.

Zoey started. For a man as solid as he was, she hadn't expected him to walk so silently.

He slid his arms around her waist. Zoey leaned against him, his fresh scent wrapping around her. "You have a beautiful home, Dex."

"Thank you," he whispered against her ear, his voice causing her stomach to turn to mush. She felt him touch her hair, the delicious sensation sending tingles down her spine. "Your hair isn't completely dry," he said.

"There wasn't a dryer in the bathroom," she replied.

"Let's remedy that." He released his arms and stepped away. Zoey felt the loss of his touch. Dex headed to a different section of the house and returned a few minutes later with a hand dryer. He slipped his hand over hers and led her back to the guest room and motioned for her to sit on an ottoman that was positioned close to the wall.

Zoey sat down. Dex plugged the dryer into the wall behind her and began to blow dry her hair.

"I can do it myself," she protested.

Dex shook his head. "Let me do it for you. Just relax and enjoy it."

Even though Zoey had dried her hair a million times, it felt wonderful to have Dex help her with it. By the time he was done, she'd had a wonderful head massage and her hair felt nice to touch. "Is there anything you can't do?" she said. "You're so talented."

"Probably not as talented as my brothers." Dex led her back to the kitchen, where he placed some chicken vegetable soup and coffee in front of her as she sat on one of the kitchen stools. Dex took the seat next to hers. "Eat," he said.

Zoey took a spoonful of the soup and shook her head in wonder. "This is so tasty. Like I said before, you're definitely talented. Maybe even more than your brothers."

"That's a kind thing to say."

"It's true."

"I'm dyslexic, you know."

Zoey's mouth hung open. She never would have guessed.

"Of course, I've come a long way from how I used to be," Dex said. "But it was a long, hard road."

That even made him more special in her eyes. "So you feel you're not as accomplished as your brothers because you had to overcome challenges to become who you are?"

Dex nodded. "Numbers come easily to Jax, for example, and Rex was practically the horse whisperer."

"Rex is the one that lives in another state, right?"

"Yes."

"But why do you sound so sad when you mention his name?"

"I guess I miss him. Rex is Jax's twin. He'd always had a crush on Tammy—that was the name of the lady Max was engaged to marry at the time—but I never thought anything would come of it. Tammy had seemed so excited about her upcoming wedding with Max, and she'd thrown herself into planning it. So imagine our shock when she jilted Max at the altar, leaving a note that said she'd skipped town with one of the temporary ranch hands.

"Then the rumors started circulating through town that Tammy had actually run off with Rex. Different folks recalled seeing them together that day. I didn't want to believe it, and I still don't now, but Rex disappeared the same day she did and has never been back since. It was a hard experience for Max to get through, imagining his own brother had stabbed him in the back."

Dex grabbed a towel and began to wipe the surface of the kitchen counter. "But as a family, we've chosen not to believe what everyone says. Rex was funny and a little hot-headed, but his heart was always in the right place. He loved us. I believe there's another hidden story about what happened that we don't know about, but Rex has refused to say anything about it. He only reaches out to Jax occasionally so we know he's okay, but otherwise, he stays away. And he rebuffs any attempt we make to connect with him."

Zoey reached out and placed her hand over his. "I'm sorry," she said.

"It's okay. Jax was the one most affected by it, with Rex being his twin. It was like he'd lost his best friend. We've learned to deal with it, but sometimes I wish he could just come home."

"It's going to be alright," she said.

Dex nodded. "I know it will. Like I was saying, Rex is a genius with horses, and Max is great at everything. It was hard growing up with all the teachers constantly comparing me to them."

"So that's why you feel you don't measure up?"

Dex shook his head. "I used to feel that way but not anymore. It's one thing to recognize that my brothers are more talented than me, it's another to believe I'm inferior to them, which I'm not. Of course, I'm reminded of it whenever I struggle to learn something new, but I've accepted that God made me different and special. That's a lesson my ma and Maggie made sure I learned well. I'm glad I have such talented brothers, but I appreciate who I am too."

"I wish I could say the same," Zoey said. She ate the last of the soup.

"Why?" Dex took the bowl and dumped it in the sink. He returned back to his stool.

"I'm not sure I have any other talent beyond medicine and my photography skills. I can't cook. I'm horrible at it, though I've always wished I could learn how to."

"You never learned at home?"

Zoey finished her coffee. "My stepmother didn't like me entering the kitchen."

"Why?" Dex asked curiously. He picked up her mug as well and dropped it in the sink.

Zoey stayed silent. It had hurt that first time many years ago when her stepmother had spelled it out, and it still hurt any time she thought about it.

"Let's go sit on the sofa," Dex said. Soon they'd snuggled up on the couch, a blanket thrown over their legs, and his arm over her shoulders.

Zoey let out a sigh. She'd kept it bottled up for so long she wasn't sure where to begin. "It's complicated."

"You don't have to talk about it if you don't want to," Dex said. He gave her shoulder a squeeze.

Zoey tucked her head further against his chest. "I always felt like the odd woman out," she said. "Like my father had formed this brand-new family and had forgotten about me. My stepmother made that message extra clear."

"I'm sorry."

"It's okay. I'm used to it now, and it taught me to be independent. But it made me long for a good relationship. Yet whenever I started one, someone always managed to mess it up. It got to the point where I stopped bothering. This is my first relationship in a very long time."

"Well, I'm not going anywhere, and I could teach you how to cook this week, starting tomorrow. You could come over, or I could pick you up and we could practice here."

Zoey looked into his eyes. "Aww, that's so sweet of you. Thank you."

"You're welcome." Dex gave her a light kiss on the forehead.

"But what about the ranch work?"

"Most of the repairs have been done, and Fred can handle the rest. I can afford to take a few days off."

"Okay. I look forward to it."

"Good. And I think your clothes might be ready now," Dex said.

"That quick?" She was enjoying his warm embrace and didn't want to let go.

"You stay here while I get them." Dex got up and headed in the direction of the laundry room, his long legs eating up the distance. Then he returned with her clothes all folded up.

Zoey shook her head and smiled. Dex was so domestic. Who would have thought? And she didn't mind one bit. In fact, it was a blessing for her.

"Give me a few minutes to change," she said.

"Just leave my clothes in the guest room," Dex said.

Zoey went to the guest room and then came back in her own clothes, all warm and dry. "I think it's time I returned to the B&B," she said. "I had no idea it was so late."

Dex came forward and wrapped her in his arms. "I'll miss you," he said.

"I'll miss you too." It was true. Zoey felt warm and safe in his arms and wished she didn't have to leave.

She'd found her own gentle giant, and she prayed no one would come between them.

Zoey parked her car curbside and got out. She was lucky she'd found the spot, as she didn't relish the idea of dropping off the car in the parking lot this late in the night and walking back alone. Dex had offered to escort her back, but Zoey had declined. She could manage on her own.

She still couldn't believe how wonderful the time she'd spent with Dex had been. Dex had character and depth but was open and quick to express what was on his mind. She'd seen so many new sides to him, and she loved them all. Of course, that didn't mean he was perfect by any means, but who was? He was special in his own way, and she considered herself lucky to have him in her life.

Did this mean she was going to accept Max's offer? It would be tough to maintain a long-distance relationship between them if she ended up taking the offer in either Boston or New York. But what if she went with the ER Center, and the relationship between Dex and her changed? Would she regret it?

No, because getting to know Dex and seeing where this would lead was worth it. Besides, she'd already had the lawyer draw up a counteroffer that minimized the risk she feared, but she'd held off from sending it because she'd wanted to see first how the other hospitals would react to the counteroffers she'd made.

So her mind was made up. She would send off her response to Max tomorrow. If he agreed to her terms, Zoey would accept his final offer. This was a decision she was happy with, getting the best of both worlds.

Zoey hummed to herself as she climbed up the front stairs of the B&B. Her life couldn't be better right now.

"Hello, Zoey," a familiar voice said.

Zoey froze. *No!* It couldn't be. *Not now.* It had to be a trick.

She turned in the direction of the voice, and sure enough, the figure she knew, the one that had tormented her over the years, stepped out from the shadows.

Dread coiled in Zoey's stomach, and a familiar taste of bitterness tinged her mouth.

The last person she'd wanted to see had just arrived.

"What are you doing here?" Zoey said in a voice that barely concealed her anger.

The figure chuckled. "Not happy to see me, sis?" Kate, her stepsister, long-time nemesis, and self-proclaimed bitter rival stood in front of her.

Everything in Zoey's life had gone wrong from the day her stepsister had arrived. Zoey had been looking forward to gaining a sibling, something she'd never had but craved. Kate was supposed to be a few years younger than her, so Zoey had hoped they'd be friends. But she'd had no idea that was the day her father would cast her aside in favor of her stepmother and stepsister.

From that day on, Kate had been given everything, but it was never good enough for her. She only wanted whatever Zoey had. If she couldn't have it, she would destroy it. When Zoey complained to her father, he never really addressed the issue or was too busy to deal with it. So Zoey had bided her time and waited for when she would graduate high school and leave the family behind. Because paying for her college and subsequent medical school was the one promise her father had agreed to.

Kate and her stepmother tried everything to make her father break his word. But it had been a promise he'd made to Zoey's mom on her deathbed and was ironclad as far as he was concerned.

Zoey had been relieved when she'd finally started college and had hoped she'd put the past behind her. The first few years had been peaceful, blissful even. But then Kate had shown up. She'd interfered in any relationship Zoey had to the point that Zoey had lost count how many times her heart had been broken. Kate had even taken away her most recent relationship with a fellow doctor who'd been getting ready to propose to Zoey. Instead, Kate had ended up engaged to him. That had been the final straw, and Zoey had lost interest in relationships ever since.

And now she was here. Just as Zoey had started dating again. But this time around, Kate wasn't going to get her way. Dex was very important to Zoey, and she wasn't going to allow Kate to screw up what she had.

"I said, what are you doing here?" Zoey repeated. "How did you find me?"

"No need to get all worked up, sis," Kate said, leaning against the stair railing. "I called your friend Tara, and she told me."

"You mean you threatened her." There was no way Tara would have given up that information easily —she knew about Zoey's history with Kate. Kate must have held something over her to make her spill the beans, though Zoey couldn't imagine what.

"Whatever works. It doesn't make a difference. I missed you, and I came to see how you're doing."

"You can go back now. I'm fine, as you can see." Zoey turned to head into the B&B.

"I broke up with Sam," Kate said from behind her in a bored tone. Sam was the doctor Zoey had almost married.

Zoey felt a jab of pain in her heart, though she shouldn't have been surprised. When had any one of Kate's relationships ever lasted? It was the same pattern with Kate: breakup, track Zoey down, find out who her new boyfriend is, try to get him to break up with Zoey, date him instead, and then another breakup. Before long, the cycle would repeat itself.

"I'm tired, and I'm going to bed." Zoey unlocked the entrance. She didn't have time for Kate's antics.

"I need you, Zoey. I need my big sis to help me with my broken heart," Kate said.

Zoey ignored her and opened the door.

"I'll be in town, and I'm not going anywhere for the next few days," Kate called after Zoey.

Zoey shut the door behind her. She fought the urge to lean against it, as she was sure Kate would make out her silhouette if she did.

Instead she hurried up the stairs and into her room.

Zoey had a feeling things were about to get worse.

CHAPTER 26

Zoey slept fitfully, and even though she woke up late in the morning, she had dark circles under her eyes. Memories of Kate's past intrusions in her life had invaded her thoughts and even her dreams. How was she going to deal with Kate? She needed to get her out of Dexin Valley as soon as possible.

She had to make sure Kate never met Dex. It was the only way. She couldn't afford to lose him. Kate had a history of fighting dirty when she wanted any man Zoey had in her life and would weave half-truths and lies so expertly it became hard for anyone not to believe them.

Zoey sat up and grabbed her phone from where it had been charging and dialed Dex's number. It rang once and then he picked up. "Hello, Zoey," he said. "How are you?"

The sound of his cheery voice seemed to calm her. "I'm good. And you?"

"Great. Absolutely fantastic."

"Well, I just wanted to let you know I won't be able to come over today. For the cooking lesson, I mean."

"Why? Is everything alright?"

Zoey could hear the concern in his voice. Honesty was another element that was important to Zoey in a relationship, and she couldn't lie to Dex. "My sister is in town for a few days."

"Is that Zoey?" Becca asked from the background. Now Zoey could hear other voices too.

"Yes," Dex said to her.

"Hello, Zoey," Becca said. It seemed she had taken over the phone. "We decided this morning to have a cookout. Dex mentioned you had a long day yesterday, so we planned to call you once we had almost everything set up. You'll be here, right?"

"I'm sorry, I won't be able to make it. My sister is in town," Zoey replied.

"Bring her here," Becca said. "You are both more than welcome. Please say yes."

"I don't think—"

"Chloe has been asking for you a lot. Please don't say no. I'll be expecting you. See you soon."

"Hello?" It was Dex back on the line.

"Yes."

"I'm sorry. I had no idea Becca was right behind me."

"No problem."

"You don't have to come, though it would be nice to see you. And Chloe has really been going on and on about you, driving Becca up the wall. That's another reason for the cookout: to help Becca relax."

Zoey ran a hand through her hair. This was really the worst timing, but how could she say no to Chloe?

"I'll be there," she said finally.

"Thank you," Dex said in a relieved tone. "I look forward to meeting your sister too. Would you like me to pick you guys up?"

And get Kate to see the relationship she had with Dex? Because there was no way Dex wouldn't want to give Zoey a kiss or a hug when he arrived. "No, we'll find our way there," she replied.

"See you soon, babe."

But even the endearment was not enough to take away the worry in Zoey's heart. "Bye," she said. She ended the call.

Zoey collapsed back on her bed. At least no one

else in his family knew about her relationship with Dex, so the news couldn't accidentally leak.

Now that she had no choice but to bring Kate along, all she had to do was keep their visit short and sweet, and make sure her sister stayed as far away as possible from Dex at the cookout.

That shouldn't be too hard, right?

CHAPTER 27

"Hello! Nice to meet you all. I'm Kate," her sister said in her sweetest voice as Zoey introduced her to Dex and his family on the cobblestone section of the main house's back-yard, where the cookout had been set up. There was a barbecue area on one side, tables and chairs set up under umbrellas, and some lounge chairs for anyone who chose to relax in the sun.

Zoey had found Kate waiting outside the B&B like she'd expected. She'd seen a flash of surprise in Kate's eyes when she'd invited her along. But that look was now long gone, and Kate was back to her old self.

"Nice to meet you too," Becca said as she wrapped her in a warm embrace.

Zoey fought the urge to roll her eyes. Kate's sweet tongue masked the viper she truly was.

Kate bent down to Chloe's eye level. "Hello, I'm Kate," she said, extending her hand for a shake.

Chloe stared at the hand for a moment, looked up, saw Zoey, and ran to her instead. "Hello, Zoey," she said cheerily, lifting her arms for an embrace.

A girl after my heart, Zoey thought. It was really true that children couldn't be so easily fooled. Zoey scooped Chloe into her arms. "How are you, darling?" she asked.

"I'm good. Where have you been? I've been looking for you!"

Zoey tweaked Chloe's nose. "I heard you've been harassing your mom about me."

"Harassing? What's that?"

Zoey chuckled. "You have to be good to your mom, okay? She's working hard to help your baby brother grow, and she needs your help."

"Okay, I'll try."

Zoey gave her a kiss on the nose. "Good girl."

Chloe beamed and placed her head against Zoey's chest.

"I'll take her," Max said, reaching for Chloe. "You just relax and enjoy the cookout."

"Daddy!" Chloe said as Zoey handed her over.

Zoey watched them move to one of the tables, Chloe chattering all the way. Maybe this could be her someday with her own child. One that maybe had Dex's eyes. Now why was she thinking about babies so soon? Or had having Dex in her life messed with her head? She smiled at the thought.

"Aw, you want a baby of your own. So touching," Kate whispered from beside her.

Zoey stopped smiling. 'Shut up," she said through gritted teeth.

"Kate, have you met Jax?" Becca had appeared beside them. "Come, let me introduce you." Becca gripped Kate's arm and led her away, turning to wink once at Zoey.

"Thank you," Zoey mouthed back to her. Thank goodness for Jax's personality and curiosity. He could definitely keep Kate busy till they had to leave.

"Hey, Zoey, could you come help me bring some drinks outside? I don't think we have enough yet." Dex beckoned her from near the back door.

"Sure." She made her way over and then strode through the back door into the kitchen. But she could no longer see Dex.

"I've missed you," Dex said from behind her, sliding his arms around her waist. "Have I told you how fantastic you look today, Miss Zoey?"

"No, sir, you haven't," Zoey said, playing along. A tinge of worry about Kate crossed her mind, but she cast it off. Jax would keep her busy for at least five minutes.

"Hmmm. How about I show you?" He pressed a kiss against the side of her neck.

"Not sure yet."

"How about this?" He planted another kiss on the other side of her neck.

"Just a little."

He turned her, trapping her in front of the refrigerator. "How about this?" He kissed her on the cheek.

Zoey chuckled. "Getting there, but not quite."

"Okay, how about this?" He leaned forward, his breath feathering her cheek. Zoey could feel her heart beating faster. Then he gave her a gentle kiss on the lips.

"Ahem," a familiar voice said.

Zoey jerked away from Dex, her ears all warm. How could she have allowed herself to get carried away in the moment? Now, they'd been caught, and by Kate no less. What was going to happen now?

"It's Kate, right?" Dex said with a smile on his face.

"Yes. I'm sorry to have interrupted you guys. I just wanted a drink and had no idea you were dating," she said in her sweetest voice, though Zoey couldn't be fooled. She was sure Kate was furious. "Let me grab a bottle of water and I'll be out of your hair."

"I'll get it for you," Dex said. He reached into the refrigerator, pulled out a bottle, and handed it to her.

"Thank you," Kate said. She ignored Zoey and walked out, but Zoey guessed her mind was already spinning with ideas about how to destroy what Zoey and Dex had.

Zoey's mood soured. "Let's take the drinks outside," she said simply.

Dex gave her a sharp look yet said nothing. She was sure he was concerned about her change in mood but had figured this was not the time to ask, instead letting her be.

Zoey made up her mind to come up with some excuse thirty minutes later and leave. By then, she would have stayed long enough for them to remember she came.

Now all she had to do was stay alert and keep Kate away from Dex until then.

But her heart worried it would be a herculean task.

～

The cookout seemed to be going well. Dex had displayed his master cooking skills and served up beef and mushroom burgers, marinated chicken kebabs, creamy corn potato salad, corn on the cob with basil butter, tossed salads with avocado and lemon, mini pineapple upside down cakes, and oatmeal raisin chocolate chip cookies, all downed with a mason jar citrus cooler of freshly squeezed orange juice, lime, and a splash of lemon.

But Zoey only managed to eat a little despite the spread, her eyes constantly watching Kate to see what her next move would be. Kate, on the other hand, was the perfect picture of a well-mannered lady, and Zoey caught her laughing a lot with Jax. She seemed to ignore Dex, but Zoey knew it was all pretense—she would strike when least expected.

Zoey checked her phone, and her shoulders sagged with relief. It was time to leave.

She looked up in search of Kate. But she'd disappeared! Zoey straightened and scanned the area for Dex. He couldn't be found either.

Her heart began to thud. She turned to Becca. "Have you seen Dex?" she asked.

"Oh, he said something about getting some of Maggie's special barbecue spice. He wanted to try it out on some of the kebab before it's all gone."

Zoey got up. "Would he be in the pantry then?"

"Sure." Becca scanned her face. "What's going on?"

"Nothing," Zoey reassured her. "I'll be right back."

Zoey hurried through the backyard into the main house. She heard voices coming from the walk-in pantry, and she hastened in its direction. Just as she was about to reach it, the pantry door burst open, and Dex stumbled out with Kate in tow.

Zoey's eyes scanned Dex's face and then Kate's. And that's when she saw the smirk, the tell-tale expression of glee that Kate displayed whenever she'd won. Then she noticed the lipstick stains on Dex's shirt.

A stab of pain like Zoey had never felt before shot through her heart, stealing her breath. She stumbled backwards. How could this happen again?

Dex reached for her. "Zoey—"

"Don't touch me," Zoey whispered.

A bewildered look crossed Dex's face. "Zoey, it's not what—"

Zoey didn't stay to hear what else he had to say. It was like her lungs had shut down, choking her. She had to leave to breathe.

She whirled and rushed through the living area and hurried out the front door.

"Zoey, wait!" Dex called out from behind her.

But she couldn't stop. She rushed out into the fresh air and took two deep breaths, her feet continuing in the direction of her car. The only thought on her mind was how to get away from here and get back to the B&B.

She jumped into her car and reversed. Dex was right at her door, but Zoey didn't stop. She sped off out of the ranch and onto the road that led back to town.

Soon she reached Miss Prissy's place. Fortunately, a car was just leaving the curbside spot in front of the B&B. Zoey slid in, jumped out of her car, and raced across the front lawn, doing her best to hold back the tears that threatened to fall.

She heard a car squeal to a stop a few feet away, and Zoey guessed it was Dex. But she couldn't speak to him now. She needed some time alone to process what had just happened.

"Zoey, please," Dex said.

A part of her yearned to stop and listen to what he had to say. But she was not ready, not with her heart bleeding like this.

She rushed up the B&B stairs, let herself in, and hurried to her room, where she collapsed on the bed.

Why? Why? Why? Zoey screamed in rage into her pillow. The action seemed to loosen her lungs, and she breathed easier. How could Dex have betrayed her? She curled up into herself, wanting to sink deep into sleep, a place where she could forget all that had happened, where the pain and heartache couldn't reach her. But the incessant ring of her phone tormented her.

Zoey reached for the phone, resisting the urge to smash it against the wall. Instead, she switched it off. But then the flashbacks of the wonderful times she'd had with Dex crowded into her thoughts and mind, and soon her eyes ached with unshed tears.

She'd had a beautiful relationship with Dex, but now, it was destroyed.

It was over between Dex and her.

But her heart refused to accept the message.

CHAPTER 28

Dex hadn't wanted to make a scene, so he'd had no choice but to watch as Zoey rushed into the B&B. She was distraught and rightfully so—even though what she'd seen wasn't the whole story—and now he couldn't even comfort her. His own heart felt ripped by her rejection as if a piece of it had been yanked away, but all he could think of was her and how she was doing.

He couldn't give up. He had to try and reach Zoey. If nothing else but to make sure she was okay.

Dex slid into his pickup truck and dialed Zoey's number. The call rang through. He tried again, but it was still the same. He shot off a quick text to her and waited to see if she would respond, but she didn't.

Then he tried calling again. This time it went directly to voicemail. She'd switched off her phone.

He leaned against the headrest. What was he going to do now? He stayed a while, hoping and praying she'd give him a chance, but despite a series of retries, he couldn't reach her.

He dropped his head on the steering wheel. Zoey had been deeply hurt, and it was all because of him. He should have been more careful, but he'd trusted her sister and assumed she had character like Zoey.

But it had been a mistake on his part, and Zoey was paying for it.

Dex's blood boiled at what Kate had done. What had struck him through it all was Kate hadn't even tried to reach out to Zoey while she fled, which probably meant this act had been deliberate, intended to wound Zoey.

Well, if Zoey couldn't fight for herself, Dex was ready to do so on her behalf. No one hurt a member of his family and got away with it.

Because that was what Zoey had become: as precious as family.

It was time to have a chat with Kate.

Dex stormed into the main house. He'd called ahead, and Becca had assured him that Kate was still there. He found her in the living room, sipping a cup of coffee like she was at afternoon tea.

"So this was all a game to you?" he said to her, going straight to the heart of the matter.

Kate gave him a disinterested look. "It meant nothing."

Dex's nostrils flared. "Are you a child?"

Her eyes widened. "What?"

"A child. Throwing tantrums that even five-year-old Chloe wouldn't throw? Maybe this is why Zoey didn't want to come here today. Because you would misbehave like this."

"Dex …" Becca started. She and Jax had come in from the backyard.

But Dex couldn't stop until he was done. It was obvious no one had confronted Kate about her behavior before.

He pressed on. "How could you treat yourself like an easy woman?"

She banged the mug on the coffee table, rattling it. Okay, now she was getting pissed. *Good.* "Easy woman?"

"Yes. I'm pretty sure you know what that means. You know, someone who throws herself at men.

There are women who end up in that lifestyle due to circumstances beyond their control, but you're only like that because of your own idiocy."

Kate jumped to her feet. "What?"

"Does it hurt to know you've lost all self-respect for yourself?"

She pointed an accusing finger at him. "How dare you!"

Dex arched his eyebrow. "How dare I what? State the obvious?"

"Dex, please calm down," Jax reached out and placed a hand on his shoulder.

But he wasn't done yet. Why had Kate done it? Zoey needed the truth. Then something Zoey had said before clicked at that moment. "So you were the one who enjoyed stealing her relationships."

Kate said nothing. But she held herself rigid, as if struggling to maintain control. *Almost there.*

"Zoey never said it was you, but putting two and two together, you fit the bill. How could you do that to your own sister? To someone who loves you?"

"She's not my sister," Kate screamed, her control broken. "She never was."

That's it. Let it all out. "So you were jealous of her. That's the reason, right? You wanted everything she had."

Kate's eyes flashed. "She had all the attention. From Father. He only cared about her. He never cared about me." She slumped on the couch. "He never cared about me," she whispered.

That must have hurt. Still, that wasn't a good enough reason to put Zoey through what she'd been through over the years. "You were wrong. So hear this, Kate. You'll never have me. And you better pray everything works out between Zoey and me. Because if it doesn't, I'm coming after you, and I'll make your life more miserable than you've made hers."

He didn't wait for an answer and stormed out into the fresh air before he said anything worse. He would leave the rest to his family. Hopefully, this would be a chance for Kate to rethink her ways and maybe salvage what little relationship she had left with Zoey.

Dex inhaled the cool evening air and let out a cleansing breath. But what about his relationship with Zoey? How could he fix what had been damaged?

He ran his hands through his hair. Dex had no idea where to begin.

"Are you okay?" Becca asked. He hadn't noticed she'd come outside.

He rubbed his hands over his face. "What should I do now? Zoey won't speak to me."

"First question: did you make out with Kate?"

Dex gave her a sharp look. "Are you serious? You know me better than that."

"I know," Becca said. "But Kate was a woman on a mission, and a beautiful one at that. It would have been hard to resist her."

"It doesn't matter who she is. Zoey is the only woman for me, and I did nothing wrong. I only entered the pantry to grab some spice, and I left the door open. Then the door shut, and the light winked out at the same time. I moved to the door to find out what was going on, and that was when I felt her press her body against mine.

"I pushed her and scrambled out of the pantry, only to see Zoey standing there in shock. I turned to see who'd invaded my space, and it turned out to be Kate, her sister. She must have gotten the lipstick on my shirt when she pressed herself against me."

"So what do you want to do now?"

"I don't know, but I need your help." He pinched the bridge of his nose. "I don't want to lose her."

"You like her a lot."

"I do, Becca, I do. Even more than I thought I would. So much that I'd started thinking about how to make the ranch work with her job situation, if she had to accept an offer outside Dexin Valley."

"Wow! That's a big deal for you. You must really be serious about her. But, right now, she doesn't want to talk to you."

Dex shoved his hands into his pockets. "She's not even giving me a chance to explain what happened."

"So you've fallen for her." Jax stepped into view.

Dex gave him a hard look. "Have you been eavesdropping?"

"Pretty much."

Dex didn't have the energy to scold him. "How's Kate doing?" He gestured back at the house.

"Max is giving her the fatherly talk."

"Great." She was in good hands. "Now I need to dig myself out of this mess. You guys, help me."

"You need to take the biggest step you can imagine," Jax said. "Lay all the cards on the table."

Dex shook his head. "I don't know. I'm not sure how she'd feel about a permanent relationship so soon."

Jax laid a hand on Dex's shoulders. "Beggars can't be choosers. If she leaves, she may be gone for good. Might as well take the chance."

Dex glanced at Becca. She nodded in agreement.

"I have an idea," she said.

A kernel of hope sprouted in Dex's heart. "What is it?"

She moved closer and explained what she had in mind.

The kernel of hope began to blossom. *This could work*, Dex thought.

"I approve of this plan," Jax said. "And I'll help you make it happen."

Dex's shoulders relaxed. Maybe this could pay off, and he'd have Zoey back in his life.

Because the alternative was too difficult to imagine.

CHAPTER 29

Zoey opened her swollen eyes to see the mid-day sun streaming in between the curtains.

She let out a sigh. She'd missed the Sunday morning service Miss Prissy had invited her to. But it was just as well. Now, she wouldn't have to run into Dex or any other members of his family.

She should have given him a chance to explain what happened. But Zoey had been so hurt that she'd had no room for anything else. She'd needed her space, and she was grateful to Dex that he'd respected that. But now, she felt remorse for brushing him off the way she had. Still, she wasn't ready to speak to him. What was she going to do?

And for her sister, she had no words. She'd hurt

Zoey too deeply this time around. Maybe she needed to raise the issue with their parents—she'd kept quiet and allowed it to fester for too long. But it wasn't something she had to handle right now. It could wait.

Yet she couldn't keep lying down. There had been enough crying. It was time for her to get up and make her next move.

Zoey forced herself to sit up. She reached for her phone where she'd left it and switched it on. The continuous beeps that followed let her know she had a couple of voice, text, and email messages.

She decided to start with her emails. Those would be easier to go through, and she doubted any would be from Dex. Zoey scrolled through and then stopped when she saw a message from the hospital in Boston.

Her heart skipped a beat. They'd finally responded. But was it good news or bad news? Opening it was the only way to find out.

Zoey clicked on the email with shaky hands and read it. It turned out they'd decided to meet her biggest request in the counteroffer. The professor she'd raved about in her interview with the hospital was very interested in working on a research project with her, and he wanted to meet with her next week!

This was a big deal. This professor had never

worked with a new attending before. It was definitely a career-making move for Zoey.

Zoey didn't know whether to laugh or cry. Instead, she was more confused than ever about what to do. One of her longtime dreams had just come true, yet she felt a measure of sadness. Did this imply she'd become so attached to Dexin Valley she didn't want to leave? Taking this offer would mean she may never really come back here again, given how busy life as an attending typically was. Why did the thought of that make her heart ache?

But she couldn't make such an important decision on emotions. This was a life-changing opportunity for her, and she couldn't throw it away on a whim. If she was meeting the professor next week, then she needed to cut her visit short and return to New York to prepare for a few days before heading to Boston. But did this mean she had to give Max her decision before she left? Zoey didn't know the answer to that.

One thing was clear—she had to pack up and head back to New York immediately. That had to be her focus for now.

Instead of dwelling on the man with the beautiful brown eyes who had turned her life upside down.

Zoey left the room and headed down the stairs to look for Miss Prissy. Sunday church service should have ended, and she hoped Miss Prissy had come home first before heading off for any visits. Fortunately, her prayer had been answered. Zoey was happy to see Miss Prissy's car pull up in front.

"Hello, Miss Prissy," Zoey said. She reached the foot of the stairs just as Miss Prissy entered the building.

"Zoey! I looked for you and didn't see you in church."

Zoey gave her a small smile. "I'm sorry. I overslept."

Miss Prissy waved her apology away. "It happens."

"So, I wanted to let you know that I'll be returning to New York today."

Miss Prissy eyed her curiously. "Isn't that a week earlier than you'd planned to stay?"

"Yes," Zoey said apologetically. "Something came up with work, and I need to return. But you don't have to refund the money I paid for the room."

"Oh, that's not a problem. We have a few people on the waitlist and can easily find someone else to take the room."

"Thank you."

"But there's one problem," Miss Prissy said.

"What is it?" Zoey asked.

"You still have a bargain to uphold."

The date? *Not again.* "Couldn't we call it quits at this point?"

"Unfortunately, I had no idea you'd be leaving us so soon, so I lined up a third date for you as promised. It's today."

Ugh. Couldn't Miss Prissy give her some notice? She wasn't in the best mental or physical state to handle a date. "It's too sudden."

"Just as well since you're leaving us," Miss Prissy replied. She tapped her chin. "Hmmm. I do remember all the lunches and dinners I had to prepare—"

"I'll do it." She would just get it over and done with. It wouldn't be too late to leave early tomorrow morning.

"Great!" Miss Prissy said with a twinkle in her eye. "I knew you'd keep your word."

"Who is it this time?"

"It's a surprise."

Zoey didn't care for another surprise, but it didn't matter—it would be a quick date and not one to pay particular attention to. "Alright. What time and where?"

"At my restaurant. Seven p.m."

Thoughts of a similar date with Dex flooded her mind, but Zoey forced herself to brush them aside. Dwelling on their memories together could break down her floodgates at a time when she was barely holding herself together. The restaurant wasn't the ideal location, but it would make it easier for her to end the date whenever she wanted.

That was what she planned to do, of course, after a reasonable amount of time had passed.

Because dates and relationships were no longer on the menu in her life.

Even though her heart ached at the thought of leaving the brown-eyed man behind.

CHAPTER 30

Zoey entered the restaurant through its main doors and glanced around. She'd chosen to dress up in a cream silk blouse paired with blue jeans and wedge heels. A few dabs of concealer had managed to hide the dark circles under her eyes.

The restaurant was empty save for one table and two chairs in its center.

Zoey scanned the space. Was she at the wrong location? That wasn't possible, since Miss Prissy had clearly stated the date would take place in this restaurant. But where had all the furniture and patrons gone?

She turned to leave and headed toward the door.

But then, the soft strumming of an acoustic guitar began to fill the space, stopping her in her tracks.

Zoey whirled. What was going on?

The music was soft, rich, and tugged at her soul. She'd never heard the song before, yet it seemed perfectly made for her. Who was playing the guitar? Was this supposed to be the date?

Zoey's curiosity got the better of her, and she headed in the direction of the music.

Before she could reach the area where the music seemed to be coming from, a man stepped into view, playing a guitar.

Zoey gasped. It was Dex.

What was he doing here? Was he supposed to be her date?

But Zoey still wasn't ready to speak with him, and she wasn't sure when she would be. Why had he hurt her and broken her heart in the first place if he'd planned to do something this special for her? But even though she was prepared to force herself to turn and walk away, the music enthralled and kept her rooted on the spot, where she stood until the final notes faded away.

Then she turned to leave.

"Zoey, wait. Please," Dex said. "I just need five minutes of your time."

She could already feel his presence affecting her, eroding the walls she'd erected around her heart. It was better she left immediately before she made a decision she'd regret. But then Zoey remembered how good they'd been together, how honest he'd been with her, and she knew she had to give him a chance to explain, or that would be the choice she'd come to rue.

She let out a sigh. "Okay, five minutes. But nothing more."

Relief washed over his features. "Thank you." He placed the guitar on the table and moved closer. She could see his face had thinned with worry, and Zoey had to force herself to hold back from touching his cheek.

"Zoey, nothing happened between your sister and me," Dex said.

And he told her what had transpired that day.

Zoey believed him, yet she also knew her sister would never give up. Kate might not get Dex today, but she would tomorrow—she was that stubborn. Zoey had no plans to get involved in that kind of love triangle, no matter how much the thought of never seeing Dex again pained her. Doing so would only poison the wonderful memories they'd shared. "She'll never give up," Zoey said quietly in resignation.

"I won't interfere in your relationship," her

sister's voice said out of nowhere. Zoey turned to see Kate coming through the main doors.

"I'm sorry, Zoey," she said, coming to a halt in front of Zoey.

Zoey shook her head in disbelief. The earth's axis must have turned on its head if Kate was apologizing. "Are you for real?" she asked Kate. "I hope this isn't a joke."

"If I wasn't serious, I'm pretty sure Becca and Jax would skin me alive," Kate said. "You probably don't believe me, but I'm sorry for all the hurt I've caused you over the years."

"Why did you do it?"

"I was jealous of you."

Zoey looked at her in surprise. "Me? You had everything."

"Except what mattered," Kate replied.

"What do you mean?"

"You had Father's love one hundred percent. It was like Mom and I never mattered."

Zoey scoffed. "That's ridiculous. I never heard Father speak an unkind word to you guys. Not once."

Kate gave her a resigned smile. "Father is not a terrible person, but giving me money and everything I ask for is not the same as love. He took note of everything you did, but he never paid any real attention to me. He broke the promise he made to me when he came to marry my mom, his word that he would treat me as his own. That he'd be the father I never had. You were supposed to be my big sister, and yet you never even noticed or spoke out about it."

What was Kate talking about? "Father always had time for you both, but never for me. I thought he loved you more."

"It might have seemed like he was spending time with us. He'd physically be there, yet he'd be preoccupied with work and never really listen. But Father tracked every award, every competition, and every exam you passed. He had all these albums in his office where he filed any news about you, but he didn't even have one in my name. You were always his first and only. There was no room for me. I thought he would finally notice me if I went after what belonged to you. But he never did, and yet I kept hoping like a fool, time after time. I know it's not an excuse for every shitty thing I've done, and I'm sorry."

"I had no idea. About Father, I mean. I'm sorry too."

"But you also have to know that none of those previous guys in your life deserved you. Of all the men I'd moved in on, Dex was the first one to resist me. I'm sure you know more than I do what kind of person he is, and what that says about him."

In that moment, Zoey felt ashamed of herself for not trusting Dex, and for allowing her past experiences to affect what they had together. How could she look him in the eye now?

"Zoey." Dex reached out and turned her to face him.

"I'm sorry, Dex," she said, her eyes brimming with tears. "I should have—"

'Shh. It's not your fault."

"I'm truly sorry, Dex."

"Are you very sorry?"

"Yes."

"Very, very, very, sorry?"

"Yes."

"Sorry enough to accept my ring and marry me?"

Zoey's head shot up. "What?"

Dex went down on one knee and produced the most beautiful diamond ring Zoey had ever seen. It was simple and wonderful and perfect. "Please say you'll marry me, Zoey. Of course, we can date and be engaged for as long as you like."

Zoey gasped. It was all so sudden. Marriage was a step she'd never imagined, but it also felt very right. Even her work situation and all her other fears no longer seemed as daunting as before. They'd still have to figure out where she'd work, but Dex had always shown her it was about her. She could trust they would make the best decision for them together. Her heart seemed to agree.

"Yes," she said. "I'll marry, be engaged, and date you for as long as we like. And not necessarily in that sequence."

Dex chuckled and swept her off her feet, twirling her around.

Zoey laughed. "Put me down, you big oaf."

Dex dropped her gently on her feet and then stared into her eyes. "I love you, Zoey Brown," he said.

"I love you, Dex Dexin," Zoey said. And she meant it too.

Dex leaned forward and gave her a gentle kiss full of promise, love, and a wonderful future together.

The sound of clapping filled the room as other members of the Dexin family filled the space, but Zoey barely registered their congratulations.

All her focus remained on Dex.

She'd come to Dexin Valley on vacation but had instead found the one man that loved her completely.

She'd finally come home.

"Hey, Zoey, do you have a minute?"

It'd been a few days since Dex's surprise proposal, and life couldn't have been better. Dex had encouraged her to take the trip to New York and then go see the professor in Boston, which Zoey had done. And now she had returned. She'd ended up keeping her room at the B&B and had extended her stay instead.

Zoey still hadn't made a decision about Max's offer, but Dex had encouraged her to take her time to think it through. She'd promised to get back to the Boston hospital in a week, which coincided with the time she had to respond to Max's offer. Zoey and Dex had discussed the pros and cons of joining the Dexin ER Center, and Dex had left the final decision to her.

She loved that he was willing to go with whatever hospital she ended up choosing—he'd assured her he'd make it work no matter what.

Dex hadn't heard back about the mentee opportunity, but they still had a couple of weeks before the Weston Brothers would officially announce their selection.

Zoey looked up from where she'd been rubbing down Lexi. It had been a miracle, but Lexi had finally allowed her to come close, though she still glared at Dex whenever he drew near. It surprised Zoey when Lexi had taken to poking her from behind anytime she reached Bella's stall. Lexi must have been jealous of all the attention Bella had been receiving.

"I'll be right there," she hollered back.

Zoey patted Lexi one more time and then stepped out of her stall, locking it firmly behind her. It wasn't above the horse to spring the lock and take off, requiring half the staff on the ranch to pursue and bring her back.

She soon reached the barn entrance where Dex stood, blocking the doorway.

"What's going on?" she said.

"I need you to close your eyes."

"Why?"

"Just do it."

"Okay." She shut her eyes.

"Keep them closed, Zoey. No peeking."

Zoey chuckled. He'd known she would try. "Okay, okay. I'm keeping them shut."

One minute passed. Then two.

"What's going on, Dex?" she asked.

"You can open them now."

Zoey did and then froze. She clapped a hand over her mouth.

Dex was standing in front of her, holding onto the reins of a Marwari horse with the tell-tale inward-facing ears.

"Oh my goodness. How?" Marwari horses were rare breeds—it must have taken a lot of effort to track this one down.

Dex grinned. "I sent out the request through my network and found her after a lot of searching. Her name is London."

"London?"

"Heard she was a bit headstrong."

Zoey chuckled. She was so beautiful. She reached out and touched her mane.

"But there's one more thing that's special about her," Dex said.

She glanced at him. "What?"

"She's Lily's daughter."

Zoey's heart skipped a beat. "You mean…?"

"Yes, your Lily's daughter," Dex said. "She's your engagement present, Zoey."

Zoey didn't know whether to cry or laugh. Instead, she flung her hands around his neck. "Thank you," she whispered.

She loved this man with all her heart, and she thanked God daily for bringing him into her life.

Indeed, this Doctor had found love with her Cowboy Blind Date.

Zoey hadn't expected it, but she and Dex ended up as part of the official bridesmaids and groomsmen respectively for Alicia, Jasmine, and Dana's wedding.

Becca had managed to pull off the wedding of the year—the triple wedding at the Dexington estate had been the most organized and prettiest wedding Zoey had ever seen.

Maggie and Peter had dropped in for the wedding before starting the second leg of their honeymoon. Dex had asked where they were going next, but Maggie had said that Peter was keeping it a secret.

Zoey had decided to stay and work at the Dexin ER Center—Max had sweetened the deal and given her everything she'd asked for. She was staying at Miss Prissy's B&B and planned to stay there until she got married. Miss Prissy was over the moon at their relationship and was already using their story as a testimonial for her matchmaking business.

Dex had bought a house for Zoey in Dexington city for her to use whenever she needed it for work, though their primary base would remain at Dexin Ranch.

Zoey and Kate were getting to know each other all over again. This time Zoey was the one chasing away the bad guys. They had a long road ahead of them, but Zoey was happy with the progress they'd made.

It had been a wonderful couple of weeks.

But now the reception was drawing to a close.

Dex grabbed Zoey's hand and hurried back into the massive house that was the Dexington legacy. Zoey had been surprised to learn that the Dexins and Dexingtons were distant cousins.

"Where are we going?" she asked.

"You'll see," Dex replied.

They soon reached a little alcove near the foyer, and Dex pulled Zoey into it. Then he began to kiss her.

Zoey sighed with contentment. She could never get tired of Dex's kisses.

"What are you folks doing here?" a voice interrupted.

Zoey and Dex jumped apart. It was only Jax with a silly grin on his face.

"What's wrong with you?" Dex asked.

"Sorry. I didn't know this was the kissing zone," Jax said. "At least you are not as bad as those guys." He pointed to Max and Becca, who'd entered the living room from the direction of the French double doors that led to Blake's study. Max's hair was all spiky, and his tie was askew. Clearly, Becca's pregnancy wasn't a deterrent in any way.

Zoey chuckled. This was truly ridiculous. Maybe it was the vows during the ceremonies that had triggered this effect in all of them.

"You need your own wife," Dex said.

Jax shuddered at the thought. "No, sir. That ain't my cup of tea."

A bell chimed through the house. "I'll get it," Jax said and strode to the door. The main house was off-limits to the wedding guests, and the Dexingtons were still busy at the wedding venue.

Jax opened the door and then froze like he'd seen a ghost.

"Who is it?" Dex asked.

Jax took a couple of steps back, and soon a face came into view.

Dex gasped. "Rex?"

Thank you so much for reading! Want to know how Rex found love (in an enemies-to-lovers romance)?

Check out A DOCTOR ENEMY FOR THE COWBOY at https://dobidaniels.com.

Or want to know what happens next in Dexington? Sign up now at https://dobidaniels.com.

If you've loved reading A Doctor Blind Date for the Cowboy, Dobi would be grateful if you could spend a few minutes to leave a review (as short as you like) on the book's page on your favorite retailer. Your review would help bring it to the attention of other readers. Thank you very much.

Check out all Dobi Daniels books at
https://dobidaniels.com

ACKNOWLEDGMENTS

Writing a book is harder and more rewarding than I could have ever imagined. And it would not have been possible without the support, love, and encouragement from my number one cheerleader, my dearest mom. My life would never have been this awesome and wonderful without you.

Of course, I have to thank my precious little DC for his smiles and antics. You brighten my day and give me the strength to keep pushing through.

Thank you to my sisters for encouraging me on this wonderful journey. And a special thanks to my baby brother (who is so not a baby anymore) for being super supportive and checking in on my progress. You guys are the best.

Thank you to my wonderful author friends. You know who you are. Your selflessness and willingness to share what you know has made my writing journey smoother and an exciting one. And a special thanks to my ARC readers whose support have made a difference.

Most of all, I want to thank God who gave me life, surrounded me with the most wonderful people, and loved me all the way. You make my life complete.

And finally, a special thanks to all my readers whose love of my stories spur me on to write more. Thank you!

ABOUT DOBI DANIELS

As a former physician and business executive in another life—with a childhood filled with reading multi-genre novels—Dobi Daniels loves to write sweet thrilling romance stories with heart. She enjoys dreaming up everyday characters who rise above unfavorable circumstances to overcome incredible odds and find joy along the way.

When not writing, Dobi can be found binging K-dramas and ice cream with her little sidekick by her side.

A Doctor Blind Date with the Cowboy is the first book in A Cowboy Loves the Doctor Series. Sign up at dobidaniels.com to be notified when the next Dobi Daniels book comes out!

Thank you!